Lex - 9

DISCARDED

The Bunker
on
Edelweiss
Mountain

The Bunker

on

Edelweiss
Mountain

Siegfried R. Hamisch

Pentland Press, Inc.
www.pentlandpressusa.com

PUBLISHED BY PENTLAND PRESS, INC.
5122 Bur Oak Circle, Raleigh, North Carolina 27612
United States of America
919-782-0281

ISBN 1-57197-282-X
Library of Congress Control Number: 2001 131179

Printed in the United States of America

For my daughter, Meika, and my little white feathered friend, Gabby. You both made my life a happier adventure.

Prologue

Bunker: A fortified chamber mostly below ground level, built of reinforced concrete and usually provided with embrasures.
—*Webster's Third New International Dictionary*

Strange things happened in Germany during those last hectic days of the war. The Luftwaffe had been shot out of the skies of Europe, or its planes parked, out of fuel, beside the Autobahns they used for landing strips. The Wehrmacht was being mauled, and teenaged boys were rushed to defend bridges, only to be wiped out, as were the old men of the Volksturm who stood in the anti-tank ditches dug around the villages in the Rhineland, helpless to stop the onslaught of Allied armor. The Allies were racing to reach the Elbe River to link up with their eastern ally, the Russian army. The end of the war was in sight. Germany was kaputt.

But there were hard heads in the German high command who still had hopes of, if not winning the war, at least of holding out until some kind of a deal could be made with the Allies, a ceasefire that would spare Germany the humiliation of total defeat.

A few of these hard heads planned to pull troops into the Alpine Redoubt, an area of mountains in Bavaria and the neighboring country of Austria. There, they thought, they had a chance of achieving their goal.

A Waffen SS general, on his own initiative, selected a beautiful mountain near the border with Austria where he would defend the *Reich* to the last of his men, if necessary. He ordered the building of a system of fortifications with which he hoped to hold off the Allied advance. He chose Edelweiss Mountain, near the village of Bergdorf, just across from the Austrian border.

The building of the concrete and steel fortification was begun in secret. But Allied solders swept through the area so fast, only one bunker, a command bunker, was ever finished.

It was never occupied. The war ended and an uneasy peace settled over the unhappy land.

Not many of the Germans in Bergdorf knew of the bunker—at least, I never heard them talk about it. It well may be they were just happy that Bergdorf had not suffered the damage that smashed Munich in the north. Most wanted to forget the terror of the devastating war.

One of the Bergdorfers who did know about the bunker was Herr Karl Schreiber, the local Forstmeister. It was part of his job as the local forest ranger to know of everything that took place on the mountain and in the dense woods that covered the lower slopes of Edelweiss Mountain.

Schreiber loved the woods and he loved his job of protecting the Edelweiss. I had seen him in the village many times, always friendly to the Americans and always glad to stop and talk to me and my German friend, Anton Brandstetter. I never heard him mention the bunker.

I don't know if any of the occupying troops in the area knew that the bunker existed. By the time I came to Bergdorf, most of the combat troops had returned to the States; those that remained were too busy with the problems of peace to care about an old bunker that had never been used, that was so well hidden on the far side of the mountain that it could not be seen from the road and trails at the base of Edelweiss.

My father was a veteran of the combat days, and now he was the sergeant major of the Bergdorf Kaserne, which housed the newly formed Sergeant's Academy, a school designed to train noncommissioned officers to carry out the mission and duties of the Allied Occupation. Students came from all sectors of the American Zone of Occupation. If Father knew about the bunker, he never mentioned it to me. Perhaps he was afraid I would go searching for it and get into some kind of trouble, an ability I had already demonstrated during my short time in Germany.

My friend Anton, with whom I'd gotten into several unhappy incidents that brought us to the attention of the American and the German police, found out about the bunker from his grandfather, Opa, as Anton called him.

Opa had lived in a little cabin up on the Edelweiss. During the war he had become so disgusted with what was happening in Germany that he wanted to get far away from the madness that was destroying his country. He found the isolation he wanted up on the mountain.

He told Anton about the bunker because Anton was in trouble with the German police and with the American military police. They thought he had something to do with the American Post Exchange robbery that took place that summer. Many cartons of American cigarettes were stolen and, as usual, Anton was a suspect.

Anton, of course, immediately told me about it. From then on, he and I had nothing on our minds but finding that mysterious mountain fortification. Our search brought us into the middle of a storm created by a small group of vicious killers who invaded the mountain hideout.

That summer the peace of the village of Bergdorf and that of Edelweiss Mountain was shattered by that evil storm.

Chapter 1

Sergeant Major Cantrell was worried when the colonel called him into his office. He knew it was about his son, Norman, and it bothered him that the boy still had the strange rebellious streak that had caused so much trouble last year. He had hoped that Norman would take a greater interest in the Bergdorf American community, not to hear that his son had refused to fire a weapon on the rifle range. He felt a flush of anger when the colonel told him of Norman's refusal.

He was disappointed, and he was sure that was also true of Colonel Dearborn. They had expected so much from the Bergdorf Dependents Rifle Team, and Norman was supposed to play a big part in it. Now his refusal to participate was embarrassing.

"They tell me Norman did fine in the basic weapons instruction, and now this. Do you think he is afraid of shooting a rifle?" Colonel Dearborn asked.

Sergeant Major Cantrell quickly sprang to the defense of his son.

"Colonel, after what be went through to save the Brandstetters on Edelweiss last year . . . no, I do not think Norman is afraid," he told the colonel. "I don't think it is fear that is holding him back."

• • •

My second summer in Germany was still young, but already I was in trouble. As usual, I did something without thinking of the consequences, and so I had embarrassed my father and myself.

This time it was the army dependents kids' rifle team. I had been selected to try out for the club. The club was the brainchild of our commanding officer, Colonel Dearborn, who thought a shooting club would help improve the morale of the dependent kids over the summer. I guess he meant well. Morale was a big thing in the army, especially in a small town like Bergdorf.

The colonel wanted me, especially, to become a member. He had sent his son, Lennis, back to the States because of some rowdy behavior and ever since, the colonel had kind of taken me under his wing as a sort of replacement for his son. I guess I was the only kid in Bergdorf with two fathers, and it was not always a comfortable situation.

My own father, the sergeant major of the Sergeant's Academy in Bergdorf, was eager for me to make good in this new club. He saw eye to eye with the colonel on the need for a shooting team. Father, always being a straight army man, was eager for me to make good in this new endeavor. Father was always gung ho. He was a professional soldier and took his job as a leader seriously; he wanted me to follow in his footsteps.

"This is a good chance for you to establish yourself as a leader of the kids in Little America," he told me.

I had other ideas. "I don't want to be a leader of anything," I quickly told him. I was an Iowa farm boy at heart and I had no great love for this military life that I was forced to live. I felt trapped by all the rules and regulations that made up so much of life. To me, the military was such a different world that I just didn't see how I fit into it.

But to please my father, I joined the club and took the basic instruction on the use of carbines and the M-1 rifle. The sergeant in charge of the instruction took me aside one day and said, "Cantrell, you've been doing great. You should have no trouble making the final shooting team. We start firing on the range next week. Good luck."

By that time I had made up my mind.

The next week I did not show up at the nearby rifle range to take part in the firing. Instead, I went with Anton, my German friend, to feed the geese at the Goose Pond in Bergdorf.

That evening, when Father came home from work, all hell broke loose in our living quarters.

"Where have you been all day?" he asked me as soon as he came in the door. "The people in charge of the rifle team tell me you did not show up for the practice firing today. The colonel is plenty peeved about you—you had better show up tomorrow. Where were you, anyway?"

He was angry. I did not want to get into a drawn-out argument with him because I seldom won those arguments. But I had to tell him what was troubling me so that we could get this over. I was sure he would laugh at me, but I had to say it.

"No," I said. "I am not going to shoot at the range. I don't want to ever shoot at anything. I just can't."

Then, words rushed out of my mouth as I told him about a pheasant hunt I had witnessed back in Iowa just before I came overseas.

"So when this hunter wounded that rooster pheasant, and the pheasant landed in our field, I picked him up. He died in my arms."

I had to stop. It was a very emotional thing for me, and even though I was now far removed from that scene, it still made me angry to think about it now, two years later. I could still see that pheasant looking at me and then closing his eyes for the last time. I still trembled with anger at that hunter.

Father kept looking at me, waiting for me to say more.

"I refused to give the dead bird to the hunter," I said. "He laughed at me and sneered and said, 'It's only a bird, what's bothering you?' I swore at him, calling him all the bad names I could think of. And I promised myself that I would never be like that hunter. I would never shoot any living thing. I would never shoot a gun."

Father looked at me for a long time. Then he put a hand on my shoulder and said: "Norman, I'll try to explain that to the colonel."

That's the last thing Father ever said about my refusal to shoot on the rifle range. Nothing was ever said again about me joining the shooting team. Father and the colonel appeared to understand my feeling, and for that I was grateful.

The team did just fine without me, but a few of the kids looked at me and smiled. I don't know if it was pity or what, but they looked as if there was something wrong with me, that I was afraid of guns.

I did not care what they thought. I was proud of myself. Two years ago I had made a promise to myself, and now I had kept that promise. That, as far as I was concerned, was the important thing.

A few days later, everyone forgot about the incident. Up in the British zone of occupation, a storm broke, a man-made storm that soon swept hundreds of miles to the south and hit our little mountain community, causing pain and death.

I heard of the Sepp Borbach escape that night over the Armed Forces Radio Network. This German prisoner had shot his way out of a British prison, killing a couple of guards in the process.

"That bastard!" Father exploded when he heard the news. His face turned hard. "He is a dirty, vicious killer! They've got to get him back for trial—he is dangerous."

I had never heard of Sepp Borbach, but Father soon clued me in.

"He is one of the most brutal killers to come out of the war. He is a war criminal. He executed British prisoners of war during the German drive into France in 1942. Then in 1944, during the Battle of the Bulge, he had his men kill American POWs. He was due to go to Dachau for trial, and now he is running loose. He deserves the rope."

I was surprised at his anger. This was not like my father. As the sergeant major of the Sergeant's Academy, he had a reputation for being cool. I think he was worried about the escape for some reason that I could not figure out. Perhaps he saw it as the beginning of another war—a little war, but still a war that had to be fought—to recapture Borbach.

I think he saw it as a storm, much like an Iowa cyclone that forms on the far horizon and, as it approaches it gets stronger and stronger. By the time it reaches you, you are in trouble if you have not taken cover.

That is what happened to Anton and me, the storm came in our direction, but we didn't see it.

And we both got into plenty of trouble.

Chapter 2

Sepp Borbach was pleased with the way his escape attempt had succeeded. "Only the bold and the brave ever taste the sweetness of success," he thought.

He was safely out of that stinking prison, he was in the farmhouse of one of his supporters. Germany was full of people who still believed that the Third Reich would come back in time, given the proper leadership.

He had no regrets over killing that German policeman and the British guard. Those things happen. Killing them was worth it because his escape saved him from the trial as a war criminal by the Allies. He had been willing to risk possible death by a bullet, it was better than the hanging by rope the Allies would probably hand out.

He looked at the new clothes his friends had provided and smiled. It was a touch of genius, dressing like a man of the cloth, a minister or a priest. The silver cross on a chain around his neck was a perfect touch.

"Now on to Austria," he told his friends. "The Americans will think I am the Pope himself."

He laughed at this. He knew bow naive the Americans could be.

"Once I get across the border into Austria, I can make it all the way to South America."

• • •

In Bergdorf the next day, I heard villagers talking about the escape. Most were excited and upset. A few just smiled and walked away, keeping out of the arguments that were going on.

Borbach had been born near Bergdorf, but most villagers were angry over the dishonor he had brought to the village. As an officer in the Waffen SS, he commanded some of the most dangerous men in the German army, and when word got back to Bergdorf of the crimes he had committed, the villagers were angry and ashamed. They were glad that the Allies were trying him for these crimes, and they were sure he would get the death penalty.

Now they stood in the streets and in front of shops, speaking in their Bavarian dialect and waving their hands. I understood a little German, so sometimes I could figure out what they were saying.

Anton, who spoke English, met me at the Goose Pond, the place where the white geese of the village swam and held you up for food.

"That was some thing, that Borbach shooting his way out of that jail," I said to him.

He looked away. He did not want to look in my eyes, something he had never done in the year I had known him. I think he felt the shame that so many of his fellow villagers felt.

"Yes—yes," he said, finally looking at me. "Sepp Borbach is well known here. Opa has told me many stories about him. Even as a young man, Borbach was bad. We don't want him back here. Most of the people are afraid of him."

Anton looked around to make sure no one was listening to us.

"It is said he has a friend in the DP camp," he said in a low voice.

The DP camp was a collection of one-story wooden barracks that housed a number of displaced persons, Polish in this camp, who were supposed to return to their native country. Many did not want to go to their Russian-occupied country, so they worked at odd jobs in the area, as gardeners or handymen for the Americans. A few started businesses, although some of these businesses consisted of questionable activities, such as dealing in the black market. One surprisingly prosperous business was the bakery, which supplied both German and American customers with some of the best baked stuff I'd ever tasted. It was always fresh, and tasted better than the stuff supplied by the army.

"We do not want Sepp Borbach in our village," Anton emphasized. "He is dangerous. He will kill to keep from getting captured. He has nothing to lose."

It was a little frightening to think that this vicious and dangerous man could be on his way to this little mountain town. Again I heard Borbach described as vicious. It was a little frightening to think he might come to Bergdorf.

Chapter 3

Frau Weidl took her job seriously. She had worked for Sergeant Major Cantrell ever since he got the house he lived in, and she had enjoyed every day of it, especially after Norman came from Iowa to join his father. Normie was so like her own son, Dieter, who had been killed during the war. This made working for the Cantrells even more important than the money she earned to support her and her disabled husband.

But now she was upset. Normie had been gone since early morning, before she even came to the house. She had no idea where he was.

Sergeant Cantrell had been emphatic.

"I want Norman to check with you every morning. He must tell you where he is going," the sergeant had told her. "We may have some trouble in Bergdorf during the next few days, and I want my son to stay out of the way."

Frau Weidl understood his concern. Norman had found his way into several bad incidents last year. One of them had almost killed him.

• • •

The DP baker came out and handed Anton two bags of baked goods for the *gasthaus* Alpen Rose, where Anton worked part-time.

"*Na*—make sure you get this all up to the *gasthaus*," he said in German. He looked at me and smiled. "It is a good you two do not work together, or you would eat all of these good things and I would get in trouble with the Alpen Rose."

The baker went back inside, and Anton left for work. I hung around the Goose Pond for a few minutes, hoping that Dorothy De Jong would show up. We were classmates and kind of very good friends, and I always felt good when I talked with her.

But there was no sign of her, so I went home, wondering how I was going to spend the rest of the day.

Frau Weidl, our German housekeeper, met me at the door.

"Normie, where have you been?" she asked. She tried to sound angry. "Your father has said you must let me know where you go, every time you go out. You did not tell me this morning."

"Ya, ya, I know, but you weren't even here when I left."

"You could have left a note for me."

"Okay, okay, from now on I will always tell you where I am going," I promised. Anything to keep her from worrying so much.

I knew why Father was trying to keep me under control. He had seen that Sepp Borbach's escape up there in the British zone could hit Bergdorf like a wild storm.

My father did not want me to be hurt by that storm.

Chapter 4

Anton Brandstetter was on every suspect list that the U.S. military police or the German police in Bergdorf kept. Every time some irregular or anti-American activity took place, they picked Anton up for questioning. But they never found him guilty of anything illegal, such as working the black market that flourished along the German–Austrian border.

One of his few out-of-bounds activities had been painting an "Ami Go Home" sign on the Alpen Rose cliff. But he had gotten away with that one because the police did not catch him doing it. His other run-in with the law had been the time an American dependent wife had offered him a carton of cigarettes for one of Opa's wood carvings. He had taken it. He wanted to give something to his father, who had recently been released from a Russian POW camp. The MPs became aware of the transaction, and they rewarded Anton with a spot on their list of people to watch.

Anton's family was poor, and he was a rebel, which did not help his status. He rebelled at the occupying Americans and for some time hated them. But now, instead of anger, he felt envy. He had met Norman Cantrell and saw in him a fellow rebel. Norman was so different from most of the other Americans he knew, so he felt that he and Norman had a lot in common. Norman was the brother he had never had.

It disturbed Anton that his father, on returning from the Russian POW camp, had been unable to find work in his field as a college philosophy instructor. He had to take on the job of woodcutter for the town. He gathered fallen trees and branches and *sawed and split them for sale to the villagers. Anton was often called the woodcutter's son.*

He hated this.

● ● ●

That evening Father brought bad news.

"Norman, we to have to postpone our camping trip for a while. I don't know how long, but until this Sepp Borbach thing is settled, we are on an alert here at the academy. I am sorry—maybe later this summer."

Several days had passed since the escape. Father spent longer than normal hours at his job, and I was sure something was up, something that had to do with Sepp Borbach. People in the village still looked over their shoulders to see who was following them, but the fear that Borbach would return to his home area seemed to have lessened.

I now checked out with Frau Weidl every time I left the house. I spent long hours at the Goose Pond, talking with my white feathered friends. It was relaxing, even though Gabby, the senior white gander, kept hitting me up for special treats. That guy could eat.

One morning I headed for the pond with a banana in my pocket, a bribe for Gabby.

Dorothy was on the pond bench when I got there, and so was Anton.

Dorothy was a classmate of mine, and since she was also from Iowa, we had a lot to talk about. She was blonde and pretty and very smart—and I liked her a lot.

Anton had a grin on his face.

"You are a little late," he said. "Your friend and I were just talking about you."

I had told Anton about my feelings about Dorothy. I hoped he had not told her.

"What are you two clowns doing this summer?" she asked with an amused look on her face.

"We've got some mountain work to do," I answered quickly.

Anton gave me a questioning look, as if this was news to him.

Dorothy shook her head. "Didn't you two get enough of that last year?" she asked. "You both got hurt—almost killed."

She knew all about the rockslide that had trapped Anton on Edelweiss, how he and Opa were hurt, and how I got banged up badly going down to get help. Everyone in Little America and Bergdorf knew that.

"Yes, we took a beating," I said. I wanted to tell her that the mountain was there and that it had to be climbed, something I had read in some book, but I did not say it. It would have sounded too corny coming from me.

"But we have work up there," I said instead.

"You are nuts, both of you," Dorothy replied.

Gabby interrupted us as he saw or smelled the banana I had in my hand. He gave me a quick nip on my leg.

As I fed him little chunks of the banana, I saw we had company at the pool. A man sat on a nearby bench and watched us closely. His face was crossed by a strange scar that made him look like he was constantly smiling. He looked away when he noticed me watching him.

Anton got up to leave. As he gathered up his bags of freshly baked bread, a Jeep rolled up and a German policeman and an MP jumped out.

"Anton Brandstetter?" the policeman asked.

"Naturally," Anton said. He sounded sarcastic but looked worried. "What did I do this time?"

"Come with us to the Kaserne," the MP said. "We have to have a little talk."

They pushed Anton into the Jeep.

"This bread. I have to take it up to the Alpen Rose," he protested.

"We shall take care of that for you," the German policeman said. "But first we must have our little talk." They pulled away, with Anton in the back seat of the Jeep.

Dorothy and I looked at each other, full of questions. It puzzled and it worried me.

The puzzle got more tangled as half a dozen Jeeps full of MPs and German police, all armed, roared past the bakery and into the nearby DP camp.

"Sounds as if they are searching the DP barracks," Dorothy said. "The DPs are shouting at the police. They don't sound happy."

"It's a raid," I told her. This was something the MPs did on special occasions. "They are looking for something. Let's get out of here—maybe we can find out more in Little America."

We hurried back to the housing area. I was angry that Anton had been arrested.

"You hear the news?" one of the kids in Little America asked. He lived near my home and knew me. "Someone broke into the PX last night and took all of the cigarettes. You hear about it?"

"Not until you told me," I said.

"Some people think it was that war gangster," the kid said. "He needs the cigarettes to help him get away."

I shook my head. I found it hard to believe that Sepp Borbach had broken into an American PX.

A few hours later Father came home for lunch. He quickly answered my questions and filled in some of the missing pieces of the puzzle.

"Someone broke in and made off with a lot of cigarettes and money," he told me. "The police think it may have been someone from the DP camp."

"But they picked up Anton—?"

"You know Anton's record, Norman. And he knows just about everything that takes place in the town. There is a chance he may know something about the robbery. The police . . . you know, they have to check out everything. I'm sure they will let Anton go after they question him."

Later that afternoon I went to Anton's home. He lived in a clearing at the bottom edge of the Edelweiss forest.

The area around the cottage looked as if a cyclone had roared through it. Piles of sawed and split wood, usually neatly stacked, were scattered around the yard. Nearby, a large pile of uncut logs was torn apart.

"They were looking for the cigarettes," Opa said as he came limping out of the cottage. He showed no signs of anger, instead, he seem resigned. This surprised me.

I was angry. In my mind the police had no right to do all this tearing apart or taking Anton in for questioning.

"I apologize for this," I told Opa. "They had no right. Anton had nothing to do with stealing those cigarettes, I am sure of that."

Opa shrugged his shoulders.

"I will not argue about what is right and what is wrong," he said. "This comes with the times we live in. These times will pass, just like the other bad times have passed. Anton is not here, he's back at work at the Alpen Rose."

Anton's mother, restacking some of the woodpiles in the yard, stopped and came to greet me.

"Will you come in and have some tea and *streusel kuchen* with us?"

"*Nein, danke,*" I thanked her. "My father will soon be home for supper. Please tell Anton I was here and that I am sorry and very angry over all this. I will see him in the morning at the Goose Pond."

That evening at supper Father said, "I'm sorry for all of that." I had made no effort to hide my anger as I told him of what had happened at Anton's house. "But the police have to check out every angle. So far they have nothing they can pin on Anton. I don't think they'll find anything to pin on him."

It was a big puzzle. The PX had been robbed. The police suspected my friend. And everybody in Bergdorf was stirred up, not just the DPs.

That night I felt an uneasiness over what had happened. It felt like the lull before a storm.

Chapter 5

He knew they called him the smiling Pole, and this did not bother him. The scar on his face came from a war wound and gave him a permanent smile.

In the DP camp, where he was a newcomer, they called him a lot of other names, but always behind his back, never to his face. He knew they blamed him for bringing the police into the camp on that raid, and he understood why they blamed him for that. After all, he had earned some sort of reputation in the short time he had been there.

He did not worry what anyone called him. Right now he was more worried about that German boy, Anton, and his friend, that American kid, the son of the sergeant major. They were nosy, like a couple of bloodhounds, and they could be headed for trouble.

And he had that worry about Sepp Borbach. He just hoped Borbach would arrive as the contact had told him he would. Then he could finish this dirty job.

• • •

The next morning, by the time I got to the Goose Pond, Anton was there. He was in the bakery, talking with the DP baker, trying to talk him out of some fresh bread for the geese.

I took a seat at one of the small tables the baker had put up in the front room of his bakery. It made the place look like a small cafe.

At a nearby table sat the man with the scar on his face. He ate a roll while reading a German newspaper and smoking what seemed to be an American cigarette.

The man looked up to me and nodded to me.

"*Guten Morgen,*" he said. "Good Morning."

I acknowledged his greeting with a nod of my head. I said nothing.

"A few more minutes and my stuff is ready," Anton said as he came to my table.

He sat down and looked at me for a long time without saying anything else.

Finally, he leaned over and said, "I have to find those cigarettes. I have to show them—the MPs and the police—where to look when something is stolen around here and not to always bother me and my family."

"Yes, I am sorry for what they did to you yesterday. I don't like it. I have already told my father," I said.

"I am going to look for those cigarettes and I would like for you to come with me. Are you willing?" Anton asked.

I did not have to do a lot of thinking about his request. After what the police had done to my friend and his family, I was ready to do whatever it took to help him. And I felt this would be a chance to do something important with my summer.

"Opa says there is a bunker on the far side of Edelweiss Mountain. He says if he ever steals something, that is where he will hide it until things cool down. He knows where that bunker sits—it's just a two- or three-hour hike from here."

"I'm with you," I told Anton. I was eager to go.

He did not seem surprised. It was as if it was the natural thing for me to do.

"We will go tomorrow. Meet me at the Alpen Rose about noon."

I had a strange feeling that someone was listening to our conversation. I turned around. The man with the scar stopped his chat with the baker who had joined him at the table. They were both looking at Anton and me.

Anton saw them. He leaned forward, toward me.

"They don't have to know what we are doing," he said in a whisper. "Meet me at the Alpen Rose. Noon tomorrow. We can talk about this then. We will have plenty of time to go to the bunker and look around and get home before dark."

"I'll be there," I promised in a whisper. The man with the scar and the baker looked at each other. The baker shrugged and went back to the baking area. The man with the scar lit another cigarette and left the room.

I waited until we were alone, then I asked Anton: "What gives with him? He scares me with that look, it's like it is frozen on his face. And he's always watching us."

"He is a strange one. He is new in the camp and he spends a lot of time here in the bakery, and I have heard it said that he and the baker are old friends. Some say he is probably a black market dealer, especially now after your PX was robbed. The other Poles are afraid of him, they wonder why the police have not arrested him. He scares me too—always smiling. I call him the smiling Pole."

Anton picked up the bags of baked stuff.

"I'll be up there, by noon," I said.

I waited around the pond for a few more minutes. There was no sign of Dorothy. I had hoped she'd show up so I could talk to her.

That night, Father was again late in coming home. Lately, his work had kept him at his job longer and he worked into the evening hours. Frau Weidl went to her home early, leaving me alone in the house.

I dug out my rucksack to get ready for tomorrow's climb. I slipped in a couple of combat rations Father had bought for our camping trip. Then I packed the field glasses he had given me for Christmas, just in case we needed them in our search for the bunker.

By the time Father came home, I was in bed. He poked his head into my room, thought I was asleep, and left.

At midnight I was still awake. My mind was jumbled with thinking about what Anton and I were going to do the next day. I worried a little about the way that man with the scar, the smiling Pole, and the baker had been watching us, but I shrugged it off.

I was awake when the shooting began.

I heard several single-spaced shots. It sounded like a carbine or M-1. The sound of the shots was answered by a sound that ripped through the night air, much faster than the single shots. It sounded a lot like the time Father fired a German *Schmeisser* machine pistol on the range behind the Kaserne.

It was scary. It was the middle of the night and a little war was going on down there at the border.

I got out of bed. Father was still up, fully dressed, as if ready to go back to work.

"They're having trouble at the border again," he said when he saw me. "It worries me. The border police have only carbines for weapons—that's tough to stand up to automatic fire."

As suddenly as it had started, the firing stopped. A strange quiet fell over the night.

I jumped when the phone rang. Father answered it immediately, as if he had been expecting the call.

"Yes—send the security patrol out right away," Father ordered the caller. He sounded very much in command. "Have them check in first with the border people. Keep me posted, I'll be at the CP."

"Nothing big," Father assured me. "The patrol can handle it. I'll be at the Command Post for a while."

I knew about the Command Post in the Kaserne. As Father left I saw him strapping on a pistol.

I had never seen him do that before.

Chapter 6

Christopher Stuart had begged for this assignment. He knew the Americans were handling most of the planning, but he wanted to be in on the capture of Sepp Borbach. He was doing it for the men in his platoon of commandos who had been captured and then executed by Borbach and his men. That had been in the summer of 1942, but the vision of that pile of men, each shot at close range, was still strong in his mind. He had promised himself he would even the score with Borbach before returning home to Scotland.

• • •

I knew that the security patrol was made up of a squad of GI combat veterans, armed with rifles and machine guns, who rode in Jeeps, ready to rush to any area to handle any disturbance. The patrol was on a constant alert. Sometimes small groups of displaced persons came out of the camp, drunk and looking for revenge against the Germans. They sometimes broke into German homes and took valuables; other times they just vented their anger and the frustration that soured their souls. It was no wonder. They had been ripped from their homes, suffered through a war, and faced an uncertain future.

The lightly armed German police, often unable to handle these outbursts, called on the American army for help. There were no combat units in the Bergdorf area, so the security patrol had been formed by the academy to deal with any crisis. The Sepp Borbach escape, followed so closely by the PX robbery, had brought a crisis situation to Bergdorf.

It was after midnight when Father came home from the Command Post. With him was a stranger in civilian clothes.

I got out of bed to greet Father.

"Everything is taken care of," he told me. He made coffee for himself and the stranger. "We have everything under control. There was some trouble when a German border patrol ran into a group coming in from Austria. Probably smugglers. Anyway, our patrol helped scare them away. That's about the way it happened, right Chris?"

"Yes, of course," the stranger answered.

"Norm, this is Christopher Stuart," Father explained. "He is investigating the PX break-in." The stranger nodded. He did not offer to shake hands. He just stared at me in a cold, hard way that made me feel uncomfortable. He looked tough and mean.

"I don't suppose you have heard any stories about the robbery about town, have you, lad?"

He spoke with a strange accent. He was not an American.

"No," I told him. "I have heard nothing."

"Yes, of course," the man called Stuart said in clipped words. He sounded impatient. "If you should hear anything, you will, of course, let your father or me in on it, now won't you?"

"Yeah, sure," I said.

There was something in that hard, angry look he had that made me shudder.

Father and Mr. Stuart drank coffee and talked for some time.

I went back to bed and closed the door, but I could hear snatches of their conversation.

"White Gander has made contact with the advance party," Father said. "He says they got over the border OK, in spite of that shoot-out with the border police patrol. No one was hurt, fortunately. He thinks the big show is coming in the next day or so. The Butcher stopped in Heilbronn for a day, but he is now on the move again."

I had a hard time getting to sleep after hearing that.

Chapter 7

Sergeant Major Cantrell felt an uneasiness, much like he had felt in combat when he returned to the front lines after a few days in a rest area. It was a heavy feeling that lay in the pit of his stomach, the tenseness that came with worrying about what lay ahead.

This Sepp Borbach case was like a small war—and it was heading for a showdown.

He was confident that all the planning would pay off and that the story would end with Borbach under arrest—or dead. He felt uneasy about one thing—he had been unable to tell his son about Operation White Gander. It just wasn't safe. Norman would discuss it with Anton, and Anton might pass it on to others, and that could blow the whole operation.

Norman had an uncanny knack for getting into trouble. He hoped that this time he would have sense enough to stay out of the way and let the professionals work to trap Borbach.

He had done his best to keep Norman from getting involved. Making him check in with Frau Weidl before he left the house should keep him out of harm's way. She had instructions to call him immediately if Norman showed any intent to go horsing around on Edelweiss Mountain. He hoped that was enough to keep his son out of the danger.

• • •

It was late when I got up the next morning. The doings of the night before had kept me awake into the early hours of morning.

Frau Weidl had let me sleep. She always had the strange idea that I needed more sleep. Now, she looked at me with the worried look of a mother.

"Normie, is everything all right with you?" she asked as I gulped my breakfast.

"*Ya, ya, alles is gute,*" I told her. I did not want her asking too many questions. "I'm just going up to the Alpen Rose, to visit Anton. I'll be home before dark."

I didn't want to tell her that Anton and I were going on a search for the bunker because that would have killed the whole thing. She would call Father, and he would confine me to the house.

"*Na* . . . you be careful now," she warned.

"*Ya, ya,* don't worry," I said. It was almost noon. I grabbed my rucksack and headed for the Alpen Rose.

I took the road. I wanted to keep my distance from the Alpen Rose steps that climbed the cliff at the rear of the *gasthaus*. The steps were closer, but they had caused me a lot of trouble last year, when I tried to climb them as a test for our Edelweiss Mountain climbing club. Everything had backfired on me, and it became one of the most embarrassing experiences of my life in Germany. The only good thing that came out of it was that I met Anton.

So this time I took the road. It was safe and legal, unlike the Alpen Rose steps.

By the time I got there, the *gasthaus* was serving the noon meal. A small number of locals and some people I thought looked like tourists sat around the tables in the large dining room.

Anton was seated at one end of a long wooden table, and he motioned me to join him.

"Helmut is making us some sandwiches to take along. I told him we were just going for a walk on the mountain. I said nothing about the bunker. That must be kept secret."

"Good, good," I said. I loved the bread roll sandwiches Helmut put together. He sliced rolls baked by the DP bakery and then spread them with cheese or liver sausage, even sometimes salami, whatever was available. As I took my seat across from Anton, I saw him. It was the man with the scar on his face, the man Anton called the smiling Pole. He sat at the far end of our table. His face was buried in a German newspaper, and he smoked what looked and smelled like an American cigarette.

"*Guten morgen*," he greeted me with a nod. He spoke in German.

I returned his nod but said nothing. It bothered me, seeing him here. Was he following Anton and me? I felt uncomfortable, I knew he was watching us.

"Have you seen Herr Schreiber, the Forstmeister?" Anton asked me. He leaned toward me so that only I could hear what he was saying. "I have not seen him today. He usually stops by here for something to eat before he goes up on the mountain. He has not been in this morning."

"No, I have not seen Herr Schreiber," I told Anton, wondering why he was so concerned about the Forstmeister. "Did you hear all that shooting last night?"

Anton was about to answer when the cook came out from his kitchen and gave him a bag of sandwiches.

"Na, have fun on the Edelweiss," he said, loud enough so everyone in the dining area could hear. "Anton—be careful up there. I need you here tomorrow. We cannot run the *gasthaus* without you." He laughed and went back to his kitchen.

The smiling Pole stopped reading and looked at Anton and me. He shook out another cigarette from his pack, lit it, and blew out a puff of smoke. Then he came to our end of the table. "So—you are climbing the Edelweiss, are you?" he asked. He spoke perfect English, with no sign of an accent.

Anton looked at me. He looked upset and did not answer the question.

"I must warn you, don't go horsing around up there," the Pole said. "Not today. The climbing is not good right now. I have been up there—it does not look good. The weather has been bad, and a lot of rocks are working their way downhill. It has all the signs of a rock or land slide. It is very dangerous."

He sounded impatient. He ground out his just-lighted cigarette in an ashtray and stared at us. He was close enough so that I could see the scar on his face and how it pulled his lips back in that ever-present grin.

"I've been up there," he said again. "Just a warning, boys. I urge you to keep away from Edelweiss for a few days. Okay?"

With that, he strode out of the *gasthaus*. His request for us to stay off the Edelweiss sounded like an order, not a friendly suggestion.

"Very strange man," Anton said as he slipped the bag of sandwiches into his rucksack.

"Really strange," I agreed. "Where does he get the idea the weather has been bad? It has not rained for weeks. I tell you, it worries me the way he always shows up when you and I get together."

"Yes, that is true," Anton said. He slipped on his rucksack and led the way out of the Alpen Rose. I followed him out into the sunny, warm day. I saw no sign of the smiling Pole.

We soon reached the woods at the base of the mountain, and Anton stopped.

"I have never seen the bunker," he told me. "Opa says it is a two- to three-hour hike from here, but I think you and I can do it faster. We will follow this trail until we reach a point where rocks have rolled across it. They are part of a small rockslide that tore loose when they built the bunker. We will not have a lot of actual climbing to do."

Now that I had a better idea of where we were going (and that I would not have to do much climbing) I was anxious to get on with the search. Not having to climb high on the mountain helped me shake off the fear of high places I still carried with me.

"Okay, I'm with you. Let's go," I said.

Our search for the mysterious bunker began. I was glad that Anton was too stubborn to pay much attention to the warnings of the smiling Pole. If the stolen cigarettes were in that bunker, Anton would find them. I was just as determined. Anton was a good friend, the only real friend I had in Bergdorf, and I did not like the way he had been treated by the police. Maybe I would help him prove his innocence, and, at the same time, have fun doing something exciting.

We picked our way along a faint trail that wound through the dense stand of pine trees and underbrush. Anton took the lead. I was sure Opa had given him accurate directions and that he could find the way to our goal.

The first leg of the walk was comfortable. We were on a gradual upward slope that was so gentle I did not even notice that we were climbing. That old fear of mine of high places still lurked in the back of my mind, but now a new worry began prodding me.

My right ankle, which had been broken last year during my fall in coming down Edelweiss to get help for Anton and Opa, was now starting to send out little twinges of pain. This was the first time I was really testing it. The dull ache worried me. I prayed it would hold up.

"Everything okay with you?" Anton asked over his shoulder.

"I'm doing okay," I said. I did not want to bother him with my ankle problem.

Anton slowed his pace and looked at his watch.

"We should be a about halfway to where the rocks come across the trail," he said. We resumed the climb.

A sound like a branch breaking came suddenly from behind us. It sounded close, and I turned around but I saw nothing.

We stopped.

"Someone is following us. I heard a branch breaking."

Anton had heard it, too, for he turned around to listen and look.

"Maybe a deer," I said.

Deer browsed all along the trail. A small stream trickled in a gully to our right. The grass grew tall along its banks, and that was a natural hangout for deer. I had seen them, looking at us with wide open eyes, ears standing straight up, probably wondering what we humans were doing in their woods, on their mountain.

We heard no more sounds, and in a few minutes we continued on a slow and careful walk. I had an uneasy feeling that we were not alone on the trail, but every time I looked over my shoulder, I saw nothing.

After half an hour of slow movement, Anton called a stop.

"Holding out okay?" he asked as he sat on the ground.

"I've got a little ache in my ankle," I admitted. "Outside of that, I'm fine."

"My leg is all right," he said, rubbing the leg he broke in the rockslide last year on Edelweiss. "We shall just have to go a little slower. We've got plenty of time."

Again the sound of a crash broke the silence of the woods. This time I could not tell if it came from behind us or from in front of us, but I was sure that someone was out there.

I took out my binoculars and scanned the area around us. The dense stand of trees and underbrush made it impossible to see anything.

Someone was stalking us, I was sure of that. Maybe someone else was searching for the bunker.

Anton looked anxiously at a sheet of paper he'd taken out of his pocket. "This is a rough map Opa made for me," he said. "I think from here on we have to keep our eyes open for rocks on the trail."

He said nothing about the noise I'd heard. I was sure he had heard it also and wondered why he ignored it.

We trekked for another half an hour, then Anton suddenly pointed and shouted: "There on the trail ahead of us . . . see that rock? That should be the place."

We hurried to a large rock that was surrounded by many smaller rocks scattered across the trail.

This was the point where we would have to start climbing the slope on our left. If Opa's map was correct, the bunker should be up there somewhere on that slope.

"Look around with your field glasses," Anton said. "It has to be up there."

He pointed to our left.

I saw only more trees, but higher on the slope they began to thin. I scanned the area to our front and to our rear, still feeling that someone was following us. Then I again focused on the slope to our left.

And there it was! The bunker! On a rock field hugging the slope, in the middle of the sprawling rocks I saw a big bulge. It looked like a huge green mushroom sprouting out of the hillside.

No doubt about it, it was a bunker! "There it is," I said and handed the glasses to Anton. "Take a look."

He studied the hillside for a long time before he spoke.

"Yes, that is a bunker," he agreed. "It is well hidden, it looks like a big rock."

He was excited, anxious to begin the last stage of our climb.

We had done a good job of finding the bunker, and I was ready to begin that final climb. I remembered that I was hungry and thought of all those sandwiches we had brought along.

"Why don't we rest a minute and grab a bite to eat before we start up there? " I asked.

It seemed like ages since we had left the Alpen Rose, and Anton was probably as hungry as I was. He dug the bag of sandwiches out of his rucksack and we began eating. I could have sat there for an hour, chewing on those great German sandwiches. But Anton ate quickly, anxious to get going.

"If we find those cigarettes up there, I will laugh at every American and German policeman in Bergdorf," he said. "I may even tell them a thing or two about finding things."

I was glad for him. I knew how important it was for him to reach that bunker and find those stolen cigarettes. I wanted to be there when he asked the police why they had not found them. And I was glad I been able to help him. Suddenly Anton cocked his head to one side, as if he had heard something.

"Down there," he said in a low voice, and pointed to the path to our immediate front.

I saw it. At first I thought it was a deer. Then it moved slowly through the trees.

It was not a deer.

It was a man coming straight toward us.

Chapter 8

Karl Schreiber was troubled. His friend, Bert Brandstetter, had his place torn apart and Anton had been picked up for questioning, all because the police were anxious to pin the PX robbery on someone, possibly Anton.

It angered him. Was it the American military police who were behind the search, or was it the often-overzealous German police? He had no idea. He liked the Americans, he liked the way they had brought a semblance of peace to the valley and the mountain. They had let him remain as Forstmeister for the Edelweiss forest, and they offered their help whenever he needed it. He had a good relationship with the occupiers. But Brandstetter had been embarrassed by the search of his home. It just was not right, this constant harassment of young Anton.

Schreiber was sure the PX robber was an outsider. The shooting at the border last night strongly suggested smugglers trying to sneak their goods over the border into Austria. Were they the PX robbers?

He would try to find out. He would begin his search by checking out the Edelweiss Bunker. That had always been a gathering place for all kinds of shady characters. Maybe the robbers had used the bunker, and perhaps they left some trace behind.

He hurried through a simple breakfast of bread and cheese. Usually he ate breakfast at the Alpen Rose, but not today. He wanted to get an early start for the bunker.

By noon he reached the concrete mass that had desecrated his beloved Edelweiss Mountain. He saw no outward sign of any activity.

He opened the iron door at the rear of the bunker, the door that led into a tunnel which was a part of the bunker itself.

The tunnel was dark, as usual, and he reached for his flashlight.

He had a sort of sixth sense that he was not alone in the bunker, but he never saw the blow that smashed into his head. He felt a second of brutal pain, then he fell. Now there was only darkness.

• • •

The man moved slowly toward us. Then he stopped.

"*Na*—Hello boys," he greeted us. He spoke in English and he was dressed in army fatigues and wore an American army issue field jacket, with the stripes of a sergeant. "Doing a little mountain climbing?" he asked.

Neither Anton nor I answered. We were still shaken by his sudden appearance. There were no other soldiers with him.

"Sit down a minute, boys," he said. It sounded more like a suggestion than an order. He pointed uphill toward the bunker. "Going up there?"

Anton looked at me. The soldier spoke in English, so Anton waited for me to answer.

"Yeah, we are," I told him.

The sergeant smiled.

"I wouldn't do that. I would not go up there if I were you," he said, shaking his head. It again sounded like a suggestion.

Anton remained silent, so I spoke again: "We just want to go to the bunker—we've never been up here before and we thought . . ."

"No, no," the sergeant interrupted. "It is far too dangerous up there. Those rocks are very loose, and if someone disturbs them, they will start a rockslide. You might get hurt. Believe me, I am an experienced mountain climber, and I would not risk it."

It sounded like this was an order, not a suggestion, so Anton and I did not reply. I was sure Anton did not like being told by an Ami sergeant that he could not climb on Edelweiss Mountain, a mountain he thought of as his own.

The sergeant noticed our silence.

"Oh, I am sorry . . . I am Sergeant Jimmy Brown," he said and held out his hand. "I am from the academy. I am up here on a special mission."

I took his hand. It was a relief to hear he was from my father's outfit.

Anton turned away. He did not want to shake the hand of an Ami sergeant.

"I'm Norman Cantrell. My father is the sergeant major of the academy."

A blank look swept across Sergeant Jimmy Brown's face. He appeared flustered, but only for a second.

"Yes . . . a great soldier, your father," he said. "I am new here, so I didn't recognize the name right away."

I was glad to hear him speak so well of Father. There were some GIs in the academy who did not feel that way about their sergeant major. Father was a well-decorated combat veteran and he had the reputation of being a soldier's soldier, but some people just could not accept that.

By now, Anton had a sullen look on his face. It was plain he did not like this Ami who was trying to keep us off his mountain.

Sergeant Jimmy Brown turned around, as if looking for someone. "Keep this hush-hush," he said. He sounded as if he was letting us in on a great secret. "I am on a mission for the academy to set up a new training area, and this would be just the spot for that. It is all very confidential, so please don't talk about it, at least not for a few days."

He looked around again to make sure no one else was nearby.

Anton seemed skeptical, as if he did not believe what the sergeant was saying.

The sergeant saw the look, and it seemed to bother him.

"You probably know that we have to get permission to use this area," he explained, more to Anton than to me. "If word about this gets out, it will just cause us a lot more work to get the approval to use this side of the mountain. I am sure you understand."

He was right. I knew that whenever the army wanted to use a building or an area for training, they had to get it approved. Sometimes the Germans complained to American military government and then the army had to put in a lot more paperwork to justify the request. It seemed likely that the village of Bergdorf would not like the academy spreading out this far on the mountain, so I could see why the sergeant wanted to keep it quiet.

But Anton, who had said nothing all this time, looked uncomfortable. I didn't know if that was because he did not like the sergeant—Anton still had a dislike for most army Amis—or he was angry only because the sergeant was setting up a roadblock to our climb to the bunker.

Sergeant Jimmy saw Anton's reluctance.

"Take my advice," he said. "Get out of here. There is one mean Forstmeister roaming this area. I have already had a run-in with him, and he gave me all hell for being up here. Had I not been an American sergeant, he would have run me in, I am sure. He is one tough guy."

Anton looked up when the Forstmeister was mentioned.

"Herr Schreiber knows me," he said loudly. It was the first time he had spoken since we had encountered the sergeant. "Herr Schreiber would never stop me from climbing Edelweiss Mountain."

Sergeant Brown did not like this reply. He looked as if he did not like Anton's stubbornness.

"I am telling you—get out of here, do not tangle with that Forstmeister," he said. Again this sounded like an order, not a suggestion. "Be out of here before dark."

He looked at his watch and frowned.

"I will see you in Bergdorf," he said and disappeared into the brush, the way he had come. It was not in the direction of the village.

I heard him moving through the brush for a minute, then it was quiet as he disappeared, headed for the Garmisch-Partenkirchen highway, which lay to our front.

"Something is wrong here, Norman," Anton said. "That story about a mean Forstmeister . . . that is crazy. I know Herr Schreiber. He is an old friend, he would never order us off the mountain unless there was something terribly wrong. And he wouldn't act the way that sergeant said he did."

"Yes," I agreed. I had been taken in by the sergeant's friendly approach, but now that he was gone, things were beginning to look different. Something was wrong here, but I could not put my finger on it.

Questions began growing in my mind. Maybe Anton and I should give up our climb for the bunker. Why was Sergeant Brown so insistent that we go back?

I looked at Anton. He had that stubborn look on his face, which I had seen many times, and I knew he would go ahead, with or without me. No Ami sergeant was going to stop him. *And no sergeant and no Forstmeister was going to stop us*, I told myself.

"Let's go," I said. "I'm with you."

I looked up the slope and took the lead on the final leg of our climb to the bunker.

Chapter 9

The smiling Pole came out of the DP bakery, shaken by what he had just heard. Sepp Borbach was arriving that afternoon instead of late evening as had originally been thought. He knew he would now have to hurry to reach the bunker. If Borbach was planning a daylight crossing of the Austrian border, he would have to be at the bunker when Borbach arrived. Borbach would never tolerate him being late. He had heard of this man's temper—he did not want to be on the receiving end of a Borbach rage.

The smiling Pole began his climb to the Edelweiss bunker. He tried to alert Chris Stuart or Sergeant Major Cantrell, but neither was around, nor was Colonel Dearborn. He hoped they would get the message he had left with the baker.

He prayed that Anton and Norman would not be fooling around on that part of the Edelweiss.

• • •

A short distance higher on the slope the trees thinned and I was able to look down the trail in the direction the sergeant had gone. I could not see him. I was thankful for that. I did not want another confrontation with that friendly but strange man.

The bunker loomed straight ahead of us. A field of loose rocks surrounded the front of the concrete fortification, as if some giant hand had dumped them on the hillside.

The bunker stood in the middle of these rocks, a green painted blob of concrete protruding out of the ground like a huge manmade rock. Some distance to the rear of the concrete bunker was a steel door that appeared to be the opening into the side of the ridge behind the bunker itself.

"There must be a tunnel behind the bunker," I told Anton. "There is a door . . ."

"I think they hollowed out that part of the mountain and made it a part of the bunker," Anton said. "We should go for the door. I think it's the best way. Those firing ports at the front of the bunker may be a little hard to squeeze through. Okay?"

"Yeah, sure," I told him. He probably knew more about bunkers than I did.

The soreness in my leg was beginning to nag me, but now that we were so close to our goal, I felt a rush of eagerness to finish the climb. The sore ankle would have to wait.

The trees gave us cover to the base of the rock pile. On the side with the door, the trees grew all the way to the door and then continued on up over the ridge above. Only the nose of the ridge, on which the bunker squatted, was completely free of trees.

We began closing in on our target when I heard the noise of crunching rock. On our right, a stranger, a man dressed in a green uniform, was hurrying toward us from below.

"Halt!" he yelled at us. "Halt . . . stay where you are."

It was not Sergeant Brown.

This stranger wore a green uniform similar to the one Herr Schreiber wore. But it was not Herr Schreiber.

"Who is he?" I asked Anton.

Verflucht, Anton said. "He looks like the man we were warned about. He looks like a Forstmeister."

The man stopped as he reached us.

Chapter 10

Heinz Holtzmann was in no mood to fool around with a couple of nosy kids. He felt uncomfortable in the uniform he'd taken from that snooping Forstmeister, and he had only a few minutes in which to get to the highway to meet Sepp Borbach.

Holtzmann knew that his old boss would be upset if no one was there to escort him up to the bunker. He had served with Borbach all those years during the war, so he knew that he could get rough if things did not go as he wanted. He had been with Borbach since the invasion of France in 1942, until his boss was captured by the British in the final days of the war in 1945. Borbach ended up being held for trial as a war criminal. Holtzmann had escaped capture and made his way to Austria. Along the way he had teamed up with that sorry excuse for a Waffen SS officer, Joachim Braun.

Now the whole Sepp Borbach mission was being threatened by a couple of kids, one a German, the other an Ami.

And that, Heinz Holtzmann told himself, he would not allow to happen.

• • •

He looked at us as if we were a couple of bad boys, playing hooky from school and needing to be disciplined.

"What do we have here, a couple of explorers?" he asked in German. He sounded as unfriendly as he looked. "Why are you up here? What are you looking for?"

Anton answered him quickly.

"We are just climbing around over Edelweiss. We often do that, but we have never been on this side of the mountain."

The man in the Forstmeister uniform shook his head as if he could not believe what he had heard. He looked impatient and angry.

"I must warn you, this is no place for children," he said with a sneer. "This is the most dangerous side of the mountain. You should not be up here without an adult guiding you. There are too many dangerous spots. The rocks are unstable and may start sliding without warning. I cannot allow this. You cannot continue on your climb."

He had switched to speaking in English, and he was pretty fluent in it.

Anton looked at me, a tight smile on his face. We'd had plenty of experience rock climbing, and this slope did not appear all that dangerous to us.

It was strange—first Sergeant Jimmy had tried to talk us out of climbing to the bunker, and now, this unfriendly Forstmeister was trying to do the same.

"*Danke*," Anton replied politely. "Thank you for the warning. We shall be very careful—we have a lot of experience in climbing through rocks, and we shall stay away from danger areas. I can assure you of that."

The Forstmeister did not like Anton's reply.

"No, I insist—you cannot go up there," he said. Anger was turning his face red. "I have told you, this is no place for kids. That is exactly what I mean. Now get out of here."

I tried to remain calm, but I was very uncomfortable.

"We just want to take a look at the bunker, that's all, Herr Forstmeister," I said.

That was the wrong thing to say. the Forstmeister glared at me and from that look I knew he hated me.

"I said no!" he shouted. "I order you both—go back to wherever you came from. Now!" He stood in front of us with his hand on the butt of a pistol he carried in the holster strapped to his waist. He kept looking at his watch, just as Sergeant Jimmy had done.

This guy is dangerous, I thought. I was ready to get out of the area, fast.

But Anton was not ready to leave. As usual, he was stubborn.

"Herr Forstmeister, we came all the way from . . ."

"No, no I have said. And that is final," the Forstmeister shouted. His face flushed. "If you continue, I shall call the police for you. As for you, young Ami," he snarled at me, "I shall call your military police. I have that authority. They will not be happy when I tell them you have resisted a German official. Now get moving, down the hill."

Neither Anton nor I moved.

I didn't know what Anton was thinking about, but I wondered, *If this area is so unsafe, why would the academy want it for a training area?* It didn't make sense.

But Anton and I had a record with the MPs. I did not want this Forstmeister to call them. They would report me to my father, and I would really be in hot water. This time, if the MPs arrested me, he would probably throw the book at me.

Anton had made up his mind, I knew that—he was going to search that bunker and nobody was going to stop him, no Ami Sergeant Jimmy and no strange German Forstmeister. That bunker was within reach, and he meant to reach it.

"Why isn't Herr Schreiber here? He is the Forstmeister for this area," Anton asked. "I am sure he would . . ."

The strange Forstmeister's face began to quiver. It was clear he did not want some nosy kid to keep arguing over an order to leave.

"Schreiber is in the Schwartzwald. He is going to the Forstmeister school there," he snapped in a tight voice.

Anton did not believe this and he showed it.

"Herr Schreiber said nothing to me about going to the Black Forest," he said.

The Forstmeister looked ready to explode. This was too much, a couple of kids arguing with him. But he forced a weak smile to his hard face.

"It came so suddenly, even Schreiber was surprised. The Black Forest school is holding a special class in new methods of preserving our forests, and he is one of the first selected for that. We are having a lot of problems with our forests," and he glared at me, "now that the Amis are here."

Anton was not convinced, and neither was I. What problems did the Americans present to the German forests?

"I do not understand," Anton argued. "He always lets my *Vatti* know what is going on in the Edelweiss Forest."

Anton was right. The quick disappearance of Herr Schreiber made no sense. I remembered Anton's question earlier at the Alpen Rose, asking if I had seen the Forstmeister. Was this, then, the reason why Schreiber had not shown up for his breakfast? Had he been sent to the Black Forest school?

Anton's stubbornness tore at the man in front of us. The weak smile dropped from his face.

"Enough," he snarled. He patted the gun on his hip. "I am now in charge here. I have told you not to climb in this area and that is all I have to say. If you refuse, I shall put you under arrest and hold you for the police."

He pulled a walkie-talkie radio from the rucksack he carried. He turned away from us and spoke rapidly in German into the radio. I heard the static of transmission, but I could not hear what, if anything, was being said on the other end.

Anton reacted quickly.

"Yes—you are right, Herr Forstmeister. We shall leave. Thank you for your warning," he said. He was strangely friendly.

I was a little surprised that Anton would give up his quest. But then, he really had no other choice. This Forstmeister meant business.

"A smart decision," the Forstmeister said and switched off his radio. "I hope you understand I am doing this because I am interested only in your safety. Now, have a nice trip back to your village. Perhaps some other day, you will be able to get back up here."

"Yes, some other day," Anton said. "*Auf wiedersehen.* Come, Norman, its best we start back."

I was sure Anton did not mean to follow the Forstmeister's orders. Not the Anton I knew, he who always questioned authority. No, I did not believe he would give up.

But he began a slow climb back down the slope, and I followed him.

The Forstmeister watched us, making sure we were well on our way before he turned and headed down to the road, where I soon lost sight of him in the thick woods.

Anton did not say a word, but I was sure he was disappointed. Reaching that bunker had meant so much to him. It had become a holy mission for him, and for me, too. We were now more sure than ever that something strange was going on in that fortification. Maybe Opa had been right—maybe the PX robbers were hiding up there. Was this strange Forstmeister shielding them? More frightening, was he one of them?

Had I been alone up there, I would have quit the mission and gone back to Bergdorf at full speed. Tangling with those scary strangers would have been enough to send me flying home.

But I was not alone. I was with my friend, and I did not want him to think I was chicken—not me, the son of a war hero. And I had made that earlier promise that I'd be with him all the way in his search. No—I was not about to back out of that promise.

The ache in my leg began to bother me again, but I pushed the pain out of my mind. I had reached a decision.

"Anton, let's rest for minute. I've got an idea."

He looked at me, a questioning look on his face. I slipped out of my rucksack and sat on a nearby log.

"We started out to find that bunker and search it. Well, we've found it. I don't think we should be scared off by those two weird guys. We should be able to go around them, approach the bunker from a different way. There's got to be another way to get up there. and I think we can find it."

"Yes, you are right about those two, Norman. There is something very strange about them. I think they are trying to cover up something."

I stood up. I wanted Anton to know I was with him all the way.

"Let's go," I said.

Chapter 11

Forstmeister Schreiber came out of the deep darkness and tried to open his eyes. He could not see, blood had filled his eyes and dried. When he shook his head it burned like it was on fire.

He tried to sit up and found he was under a pile of blankets. His hands were tied, and he saw he had been stripped of his uniform. His thirst was demanding. It was probably the thirst that had aroused him.

Then he heard the voices. They were somewhere on the outside of the tunnel.

Whoever was out there was speaking in English, and Schreiber's heart gave a little jump of joy and hope. That sounded like Amis out there, and they had found him!

Then everything went silent, and waves of darkness again crashed over him like ocean waves on a rocky shore. His last conscious thought was that help is here.

• • •

"Those two guys went on down to the highway," I said. "If we go back a ways and then climb uphill to the ridge we have woods all the back to the bunker. If we're careful we can work our way to the bunker without being seen."

Anton did not say anything for some time. Then he looked straight at me and asked: "Are you sure you still want to come with me?"

"Yes, we have come this far. I think we should go all the way."

He grinned. He slapped me on the shoulder.

"Lead the way, my friend. I'm right behind you," he said.

I began to backtrack, confident we could move along the ridge and get all the way to that back door without being seen. We just had to be careful and quiet.

Several times we stopped to listen and to search the surrounding woods to make sure we were alone. Except for a couple of deer standing among the trees, we seemed to be alone.

"I guess that Forstmeister thinks he's scared us off," I said. "He is one nutty guy."

"*Ya—ya*, that he is. He is gone but we must still be very careful. Those two may come back or there may be others up there."

We back-trekked for some time when Anton called a stop.

"We have gone back far enough," he said. "From here on we head back up the slope to get on the same level with the bunker."

He now took the lead and we moved faster. We had lost time because of the interruptions, now we wanted to get to that bunker, search it, get out of there, and get home before dark. Once we got upslope we went parallel to the ridge and made good headway.

We reached a small opening among the trees and there it was, right in front of us—the bunker! We were only a few yards from the steel door at the rear entrance to the bunker tunnel.

Anton stopped and held up his hand.

"Be careful here," he whispered.

I stopped. I listened. The only sound came from the wind soughing through the tall pines. No sound came from the bunker.

We moved forward to the steel door.

"Let's leave our rucksacks out here," I said. "If there is someone in there and we have to get out of here fast, we can move better without our rucks."

"Ya, we may have to do that," Anton agreed. "If there is someone in there, we get out of here and run like the wind for Bergdorf. We will let the police handle it from there."

I heard my heart pounding away, and I began sweating, not because of the climb but from the anxiety that gripped me. The warnings of Sergeant Jimmy and the Forstmeister were again sounding alarms in my head, and it didn't help to remember that the smiling Pole, back at the Alpen Rose, had also tried to talk us out of coming up here.

Why were they all trying to keep Anton and me from the bunker? Were they trying to hide something? Maybe they did have the stolen PX cigarettes in there. They must have, or they would not have tried so hard to stop us.

It was a puzzle and I did not have any answers, only the feeling that there was something about that bunker that they did not want us to know.

I think Anton felt as I did. For him it was now more necessary than ever to get inside that concrete box. It had become a holy mission that grabbed him and would not let go. If the cigarettes were in there . . .

My ankle ached more than ever. I had stepped on a pine cone, and the twist was enough to awaken all of the old pain.

I reached the steel door and turned the handle. The iron hinges screeched, but the door slowly opened. I stepped into a darkened space, the start of a big cave-like tunnel that began at the door and led to the concrete rear wall of the bunker. At the rear wall was an opening, the back entrance to the bunker itself. I shuffled forward, my eyes slowly adjusting to the darkness. The only light came from the opened door and from the gunports in the front wall of the bunker.

"*Verflucht!*" Anton swore in a low voice. "It is so dark . . . it looks empty."

I rushed back out get the flashlight I carried in my rucksack. I always carried it, you never knew when Father would suddenly decide to go on that camping trip he had promised me. I wanted be ready.

I flashed the beam around. The tunnel was carved out of the rock in the mountain and was divided by wooden walls into a number of small rooms. In one of the room areas several folding canvas cots had been set up. In the rear of the tunnel, in almost complete darkness, a pile of blankets lay in a heap on the stony floor. Along the tunnel wall that stretched forward to the bunker lay a number of wooden boxes that looked like the ammunition boxes I had seen at the rifle range behind the Kaserne.

Anton immediately began digging into the boxes. They were empty. They held no cigarettes. But, on the ground near the rear of the bunker entrance were a couple of rucksacks.

"Anton—there," I said and focused the flashlight on the rucksacks. "Look—there on the floor and there on the wall—a submachine pistol!"

I remembered the night firing along the border—one of those weapons had the burrrp sound made by a machine pistol.

Anton rushed to the first rucksack and opened the large rear flap. He held up papers, holding them in the beam of the light so he could study them.

"Norman, you must see this," he said, excitement in his voice, "Bring your light up closer . . . you must look at these."

He shuffled through the booklets in his hand.

"These are *Soldbuchs*," he whispered.

"Never heard of *Soldbuchs*," I said.

"They are books used by Wehrmacht soldiers. They are books that show the pay allowances and a lot of information about the bearer of the book."

I looked at the booklet he handed me.

A familiar picture jumped out at me from the *Soldbuch*.

"Sergeant Jimmy," I said loudly. I couldn't believe it. "This is Sergeant Jimmy Brown—in a German army uniform!"

"Yes, it is our friend Sergeant Jimmy," Anton replied. He studied another booklet. "This one belongs to the Forstmeister who stopped us out there."

He sounded as if he could not believe what he was seeing.

"*Mein Gott!*" he said as he handed the other booklet to me. "Look at those uniforms these guys are wearing. These two were in the Waffen SS."

I knew about the Waffen SS. Father had told me about them, of how they had been the toughest and meanest soldiers in the German army. "This looks like the Forstmeister was a SS *Hauptsturmfuhrer*—that is like a . . . like a captain in the Wehrmacht. His name is Heinz Holtzmann. And this is Sergeant Joachim Braun, our Sergeant Jimmy . . . an SS *Scharfuhrer*—a sergeant," Anton said.

"What was he doing in that American uniform?" I asked.

He shrugged.

Then it hit me.

"Maybe he stole it somewhere—hey, he speaks very good English . . . maybe he was one of those American-speaking soldiers who led the German Army during the Battle of the Bulge."

Father had told me about the German soldiers who could speak good English, were dressed in American army uniforms and led the attack against American forces. They caused great confusion during the early stages of the Battle of the Bulge. And those in the Waffen SS sometimes committed crimes against U.S. soldiers. Many had been arrested after the war and were being held for trial as war criminals. Sepp Borbach was one of these.

"These well may be the ones who robbed the PX. Maybe they need the cigarettes to help them escape from Germany," Anton said. He sounded hopeful. Maybe we would still finds signs of the PX robbery here in the bunker.

"Yeah, they could also be working the black market along the Austrian border," I said. "But I don't get it . . . the smiling Pole is supposed to be the big border operator. Is he one of them? I don't see any *Soldbuch* for him." Anton did not answer, he was busy studying a new set of papers he had pulled from the rucksack.

"Look at these—*Deutsche Kennkarten*," he shouted as he handed one to me.

It was a German identification card, a card that all Germans had to carry. I looked at one belonging to Joachim Braun, our "Sergeant Jimmy." He was not in an American uniform, nor in an SS uniform, he was in civilian clothes. It was him all right, that SS sergeant in the *Soldbuch*!

Anton gave me two more German ID cards. One was for Heinz Holtzmann, the Forstmeister, and he also was in civilian clothes.

The third ID shook me. The picture showed a face that was frightening to look at, a scarred face that looked hard and mean. There was no hair on his head. The man looked evil. I had never seen anyone that looked as vicious as that man in that picture.

The card said he was Father Franz Becker. His occupation was listed as that of a priest.

"Who is this guy? Where is he?" I asked. An unsettling thought was already prodding my mind. This was another SS officer—this was Sepp Borbach. I was sure it was him.

Anton studied the ID. "I am not sure who that is," he said. "But I think that is Sepp Borbach."

I looked for another ID card to see if there was one for the smiling Pole. Was he a former SS man, passing as Polish and hiding in a DP camp? I found no ID card for him.

But Anton had found something else. Bundles of paper money, tied neatly together.

"This is something," he said as he looked at the bundles. "These are Ami dollars, Ami scrip, German marks, Austrian schilling—everything. I tell you Norman, these are big operators."

I agreed.

"Yeah, I guess they are afraid that if they are stopped by the police for any reason, they would have a hard time explaining all this stuff. That's why they got everything—

the *Soldbuchs*, the *Kennkarte*, and the money, all stashed away here in the bunker."

"Yes," Anton said. "If the police find this, they are in big trouble. It is strange, Norman, but I do not see any cigarettes."

"No," I said. "But this money is like gold for someone who wants to get out of Germany. If they had cigarettes they may have moved them somewhere else. I don't know . . . it is all very confusing to me."

I had seen the *Kennkarte* that I thought belonged to Sepp Borbach. Maybe this whole thing was a part of his escape plan.

Anton found a bundle of crumpled clothes lying in a corner of the tunnel. He began sorting through the pile when he suddenly stopped.

"Did you hear . . . ?"

I heard it, too. It was a low, weak moan. It came from the bundle of blankets at the end of the tunnel. My heart began pounding even harder as I shot my flashlight beam toward the pile of blankets. The moan came from there.

The pile of blankets began moving. A leg and a foot crept slowly out from under the blankets.

It was a person, and he moaned again.

"Anton," a voice spoke. It was so weak I could hardly understand it.

I backed away from the pile, but Anton shot forward and began to tear at the blankets.

He tore off the last blanket and I saw the body of a man, his head covered with blood.

"Anton, *Gott sei dank*," the man said.

"No . . . oh no," Anton gasped and dropped to his knees beside the man.

I stood paralyzed. I did not want to believe what I saw. The man had been stripped of his outer clothes and he lay, hands bound with wire.

"Herr Schreiber . . . Herr Schreiber!" Anton said loudly.

Chapter 12

Anton saw the bloodied head of Forstmeister Karl Schreiber and he froze with fear.

Questions tore at his mind. What was Herr Schreiber doing up here in the bunker? What had happened to him? Why would anyone do this to him? This was like finding your own father, bloodied and helpless on the floor in front of you.

Herr Schreiber had indeed been like a father to him during all those years when Anton's father was in the Russian POW camp. It was Schreiber who took Anton on long walks on Edelweiss and taught him the basics of mountaineering. It was Schreiber who had shown him all those secret places on the mountain like the edelweiss flowers, the wild strawberries, and where the deer lived with their young ones.

And in all those years that Opa had lived alone up on Edelweiss, it was Herr Schreiber who checked on the old man almost daily.

When the Americans came to occupy Bergdorf, Herr Schreiber had helped Anton make his peace with them. It was Herr Schreiber who had gotten Anton's father the job as wood-cutter for Bergdorf. Yes, he had been there when his family needed a helping hand.

Now the tables had turned. Now it was Forstmeister Schreiber, in pain on the floor, who needed help.

• • •

Herr Schreiber kept his eyes shut, but he worked his mouth and I could hear, "Anton—*Gott sei dank. Gott sei dank.*"

His hands were tied with what looked like communication wire from a spool in the tunnel. He lay sprawled on his back.

Anton dropped to his knees beside him.

"Herr Schreiber . . . Herr Schreiber, what has happened? Who. . . ?"

"*Vasser, bitte,*" Herr Schreiber begged. He ran his tongue over his lips. "*Vasser.*"

I took my canteen from my belt, opened it, and carefully placed the spout to his lips. He again ran his tongue around his lips and swallowed the water. He rested for a minute, then gulped down more. Slowly, he opened his eyes. He looked at me, gave me a short nod of thanks, and drank some more.

Anton took his own canteen out and soaked a handkerchief with water. He placed the handkerchief on Herr Schreiber's forehead, and the Forstmeister moaned in appreciation.

He stopped drinking.

"*Danke . . . danke, das ist so gute,*" he said. His voice was full of pain. "My boys . . . thank you."

I untied the wire that bound his wrists and, with Anton's help, got him into a sitting position.

"He is very weak," Anton said.

"We've got to get him out of here—get him back to Bergdorf," I said, wondering how we were going to manage that.

"He cannot sit by himself . . . he won't be able to walk," Anton said.

Our situation shook me fully aware that something evil had taken place here in the bunker—and we were now in the middle of it. Sweat clouded my eyes.

We were in danger, that much was obvious. We had been told by three different people to stay away from the bunker. We had ignored them. Now we had found the

badly injured Forstmeister and we had to get him to med-
ical care quickly. We had stumbled into something too big
for us to handle, something the police would have to handle. But who had done this to Herr Schreiber? Was it that
guy passing as a Forstmeister, that SS officer, Heinz
Holztmann? He looked vicious enough.

Anton looked very worried. "We will get you out of
here," he said, speaking in German to Schreiber. "We will
get you back to Bergdorf. Everything will be just fine."

Herr Schreiber shook his head.

"*Nein, nein.* I cannot walk," he said weakly. "You cannot carry me . . . you must go . . . leave me here. Get the
police . . . fast."

He lay back on the tunnel floor. Anton put his arm
under him and tried to get him back to a sitting position,
but it was of no use.

"Go, now," Schreiber said. "If they come back . . . they
will kill you. They are . . ."

The Forstmeister closed his eyes and he looked asleep.

Anton turned to me, as if I had an answer to our problem.

"He is okay for now," I said. "We've got to get the
police up here. This thing is way over our heads."

He nodded.

"*Ya*, you are right."

He took a last look at Herr Schreiber.

"We shall be back as fast as possible," he told the
Forstmeister. He placed his canteen of water beside Herr
Schreiber. Then he replaced the pile of blankets gently over
his friend. Once again it looked like a crumpled heap of
blankets on the floor at the end of the tunnel. I snapped off
my flashlight and headed for the door. Anton was right
behind me.

At the door, I stopped quickly and he plowed into me.

Below us, on the slope just below the bunker, I saw a
small group of men. There were three of them and they
were on the final climb up to us.

I recognized two of them immediately.

Chapter 13

Sepp Borbach was relieved. The most dangerous part of his escape was over. Now he could rest a few days in the safety of the hidden bunker while he refined his escape operation. From here on he would have the help of two more friends from the Waffen SS who would help make the next leg of his long journey to freedom a success.

Heinz Holtzmann was glad he had reached the highway in time to meet the car bringing his commander from up north. Now all that remained was to get back to the bunker, rest, and go over the plans for the getaway and then cross the border. If they did get into a tight spot along the way, he hoped that dumb former SS Sergeant Braun would carry his share of the load.

Holtzmann sometimes felt a little uneasy about Braun's commitment to the escape operation. He would have to keep an eye on the man.

Holtzmann knew that he was in the American's automatic arrest category for his shooting of American POWs during the Battle of the Bulge. They would hang him along with Borbach. He would go down fighting before he would let them capture him. If he got back to Salzburg, he should be safe for a long time.

Joachim Braun, too, was glad he had been able to get to the highway in time to escort the former SS Sturmbahnfuhrer to the bunker. He had never met Sepp Borbach in person, and when he did finally meet him at the highway pickup point, he had felt a sudden moment of fear. Borbach was a killer—he already knew that from the stories going around about him from former combat companions—but just the way the man looked was enough to give one nightmares.

Braun would accompany Holtzmann and Borbach until they reached Salzburg, where the next group of supporters would take over. There he would leave the team. He hoped he would never again see Holtzmann or Borbach.

● ● ●

Three men were approaching the bunker. One was carrying a pistol. That was Holtzmann. Another man, in U.S. Army fatigues was "Sergeant Jimmy," Joachim Braun of the *Kennkarte*. They escorted a man dressed as a priest. He was the Father Franz of the ID cards we had seen.

This had to be Sepp Borbach.

The scarred face was more frightening in person than it had been on the *Kennkarte* picture. His dirty blond hair was cut so short that he looked bald.

No question about it—this was Sepp Borbach.

Anton and I stared, but only for a second. Then we jumped into action and began running down the slope, away from the bunker and away from the approaching men. We headed for the dense stand of trees on the lower slope, along the trail to Bergdorf.

I ran with little control. Sometimes I ran into trees or got whipped by low-hanging branches so hard I got blood on my face. I lost my balance as I tripped over an exposed tree root and had to struggle to keep from falling.

My ankle hurt. I started to limp as I tried to catch up with Anton, who was increasing the distance between us with every step.

Dense brush along the trail and the nearby gully popped up in front of me and I made a final dash to reach the cover.

"Halt!" someone to our rear shouted.

I looked over my shoulder and saw Holtzmann, in the Forstmeister uniform, closing in on us, pistol in hand.

"What is it you want?" another voice shouted in English. That was Braun.

My ankle burned with pain. I tried to catch up with Anton, but it was no use. He was running fast and steady on the way to Bergdorf.

A clump of dense underbrush shot up in front of me. I threw myself into the brush and sprawled to the ground.

"Anton—I can't go anymore," I gasped.

Anton stopped and turned. He saw me on the ground and immediately ran back toward me. He grabbed my arm and began pulling me deeper into the gully underbrush.

"We will hide here," he whispered. "Stay low, maybe they will not see us . . . maybe they will think we got away."

I tried to squirm into the ground, like a gopher trying to escape by digging a new hole. My heart was pounding like crazy, from running and fear.

"Can you walk at all?" Anton asked in a whisper.

I shook my head. "No, my ankle is shot."

"Then we will just have to sweat it out," Anton said. "Let's hope they will think we got away and stop looking."

I heard voices on the trail some distance behind us. It was Braun and Holtzmann yelling to each other in German.

Suddenly there was movement in the brush to our front and a low voice said: "You must get out of here—fast."

A man plopped down on the ground beside Anton and me.

It was the smiling Pole.

Chapter 14

Lieutenant Jan Gudowski was worried and he was angry. He had told young Cantrell and his German friend, back there at the Alpen Rose, to stay off Edelweiss today.

He regretted not having ordered them to stay off, to go home, and he wished he had called Sergeant Major Cantrell and told him to keep his kid out of the way.

With Anton, it probably would have been more difficult to order his father to keep his son at home. Herr Brandstetter might resist taking orders from what he thought was a Polish displaced person. He could not tell him why he should keep Anton off the mountain. Now he saw only one choice of action left to him, and he prayed that it would succeed.

• • •

The Pole looked angry.

"I told you kids not to come up here today," he said, his anger strong in his voice. "You are in something that is way over your head."

He saw me rubbing my ankle and he turned to Anton.

"Listen very carefully, Brandstetter," he said, speaking rapidly and quietly. "Get to the Kaserne as fast as you can. Tell the sergeant major that the White Gander is in serious trouble. I need help right away. Tell him the Butcher is already here. Got it?"

Anton was astonished and had a puzzled look on his face. He nodded.

"If you can't find Sergeant Cantrell, try Colonel Dearborn," the smiling Pole ordered, "tell the MPs—tell anybody in charge there—just tell them to get help up here fast. Understand?"

Anton understood. He looked at me.

"Don't worry about him—I'll do what I can," the Pole said. "Get going. Run like hell."

Anton shot off through the brush like a startled deer. Then he was gone.

I said a silent prayer for him—reach the Kaserne safely, I prayed, and reach it quickly. Above all, bring help in time.

This sudden turn of events since we left the bunker had me really confused. The smiling Pole had spoken to us in perfect English, just as he had in the Alpen Rose. And he had said that White Gander was in trouble. Was he the White Gander Father had mentioned the night of the shooting? He had said something about a White Gander when he spoke to that strange Christopher Stuart, the PX robbery investigator. And why was the White Gander now in trouble? I had believed the Pole was one of the bunker gang.

"Cantrell, you are a young damn fool," he quickly told me. "You are playing around where you have no business."

I heard a crashing in the nearby brush. I was sure it was Holtzmann and Braun.

"You are a stupid little fool," the smiling Pole suddenly shouted loudly, at me. "We are going to have punish you for this."

Now I was really confused, and scared.

He leaned close to me and whispered, "I'll try to help you. You will have to trust me. I'll take you back to the bunker. Don't ask any foolish *questions*; try to keep your sore ankle under control. Just act scared—and pray your friend gets help to us in time."

I didn't have to act scared, I was as scared as I'd ever been.

He grabbed me by an arm and yanked me to my feet.

"I have one of them," he shouted in German.

I now understood what he was doing. He was showing the rest of the bunker gang that he had captured one of the intruders.

In a moment the brush in front of us parted and Heinz Holtzmann, pistol in hand, stood before us. "So, you had to come back to see what is up there," he snarled at me.

He pointed his gun directly at me and for a long moment I thought he was going to shoot. I stopped breathing.

Then he lowered the pistol and looked angrily at the smiling Pole.

"What is the matter with you?" he asked. "You could have caught that other little bastard before he got away. What is the matter with you?"

"I was too busy with this one," the Pole said quietly. "I thought the other one would stay here with his friend. But he's only the son of a woodcutter, so I guess he's just interested in saving his own neck. This is the valuable one—he is the son of the Kaserne's sergeant major, and I think we can find a good use for him. Maybe as a hostage, if we run into trouble tonight."

Holtzmann's face had a look that just about killed any hope I had that I would survive this, even if they used me as a hostage.

He prodded me forward, out of the underbrush. I wanted to limp with every step, but the smiling Pole had told me to hide my pain. Why I should do this, he did not say. I bit my lip and choked back my urge to a moan, even when Holtzmann jabbed the pistol into my ribs.

My mind was numb with fear. I struggled to make sense of what the Pole was up to. If he was a member of this gang, why did he let Anton escape—and order him to bring help? I knew that a lot was happening here that I did not understand, but I was now certain that the Pole was not one of the Borbach gang.

The fear of being a prisoner of the bunker gang pushed everything else out of my mind.

I struggled slowly up the slope, each painful step bringing me closer to the bunker. And to Sepp Borbach.

As we reached the tunnel door, Holtzmann shoved me roughly into the tunnel with a push that forced me to stumble in the semi-darkness.

"On the cot," my captor ordered and gave me a final push that sent me sprawling on one of the cots.

"Now . . . you stay there or I will use this," he said as he jabbed his pistol into my stomach, so hard this time I yelled in pain.

Holtzmann grinned and sneered.

"Do as he says," the Pole told me in a rough voice.

Down in the gully he had sounded considerate, here in the bunker he was as bullying as Holtzmann. But, whoever he was, he was my only hope.

I curled up on the cot, hurting from the jab of the pistol, and sweating with fear.

I cursed the hurting ankle that had stopped me from making my escape with Anton.

"So—I understand we have a young Ami here," a voice said. I looked up, right into the frightening face of Sepp Borbach.

Chapter 15

Up to now, Borbach had been satisfied with the way his team had things under control. From here it was only a short trip to Salzburg, where he should be completely secure. True, the Amis were in the city, but Salzburg was full of refugees from the East and there were a lot of tourists crowding the streets of the old city. He would be able to move about freely with little fear of getting caught.

Now, however, he saw a new problem that could interfere with his escape operation right here on Edelweiss Mountain.

There were people in the bunker who posed a threat. There was that dumb Polack with that stupid grin. He had never liked the Polish, and he really did not need this one for the border crossing, so getting rid of him would be no problem.

As for the young Ami, Braun or Holtzmann should have taken care of him down there in the gully. But they had fumbled things down there. They had let the other boy escape, and they had brought the Ami back to the bunker.

This created a new problem. He had hoped to stay in the bunker for at least a day. Now he would have to speed up his plan and get to the border crossing sooner than he had planned.

• • •

Borbach was huge, he was tall and wide, and he looked as if he could grab a person with one hand and crush him.

He turned to Holtzmann. "And what do you have in mind for him?" he asked. He pointed at me.

The Pole quickly spoke up. "We can use him as a hostage, if necessary," he said.

"I will make the decision on that," Holtzmann replied. He sounded impatient. "I do not like the idea of dragging him along until we cross the border. You should have shot him and his friend when you had the chance down there in the gully. It would have been better than bringing him up here."

Holtzmann seemed to dislike the Pole. He made that plain in the way he looked and talked. "I will decide later what to do with the Ami," Borbach ordered. He tried to smile. "Perhaps he can carry our bags for us."

This brought a faint smile from Holtzmann.

"*Ya wohl*, Herr *Ober* . . ." Holtzmann began.

Borbach held up a huge fist and for a moment I thought he was going to hit Holztmann.

"Never call me by my former rank. I am now Father Franz. Do not forget that. Now, let's go over our plans for the next step."

"Of course, Father," Holtzmann said. He still looked amused. Maybe it was the sight of Sepp Borbach as a religious person. "As soon as it gets dark, we cross over into Austria. From the border we hike to a farmhouse at the edge of the Kleine See and meet our escort who will take us to Salzburg. In Salzburg we . . ."

"The border. You are certain we will have no trouble with that?" Borbach interrupted.

The Pole stepped forward. "There have been some changes along the border, Father Franz. The border police now send out patrols, especially at night. But I know where the police checkpoints are, and I know how to get around them. I know how to get past the patrols," he said. He sounded confident. "I have been working that area for some time, and I know . . ."

"Enough, Polack," Borbach said with a growl.

"Father Franz, we do not need a guide. I came across last night . . . I know the way well," Holtzmann said.

"Very well," the Pole replied. "But there is a new passage past the checkpoints that will get us to the See faster and with less chance of interference. I have used it several times, with good results. At the See, your Austrian contact will be waiting and take you . . ."

"What do you know about my Austrian contact?" Borbach asked sharply.

The Pole remained cool. "Father, Herr Holtzmann said . . . I met your two aides there at the contact point, so I just assumed . . ."

"Polack, we assume nothing, understand? We must plan and be sure of every step we take in this venture. That is the only way to succeed in matters like this," Borbach said.

"Of course, Herr . . . Father Franz," the Pole answered. "I just thought . . ."

Borbach turned his back on the Pole. As far as he was concerned, the conversation was over.

Now Borbach turned to me, studying me with his hard-eyed stare.

"I understand you are the son of the sergeant major in Bergdorf? So, how can you help me get to Austria?"

Borbach knew I was terribly frightened, and he wanted to play a little game with me, a game I did not know how to play.

"He is a kind of insurance for us, Father Franz," Sergeant Jimmy spoke up.

"Joachim, we must travel light and we must travel fast. There is no room for a young Ami in our plans."

"Very well, we can tie him up and leave him here along with Forstmeister Schreiber," Sergeant Jimmy suggested.

"Forstmeister Schreiber?"

"*Ya*—we caught him snooping around the bunker. Heinz . . . disabled him. He is under that pile of blankets over there."

"That Heinz . . . still up to his old tricks. Is the Forstmeister still alive?"

"I think he is," Sergeant Jimmy said.

The Pole got back into the conversation.

"I think Herr Braun is correct. We tie the boy up and leave him here. That way we get him off our hands. Sooner or later his German friend will come back here and . . ."

"*Ya*, sooner or later that other one will come back, and he won't be alone. We have to change our plan. I had hoped for a night crossing of the border. Now we can't afford to wait for darkness. Heinz, let's take another quick look at that map."

Holtzmann returned with a map.

"We cross some distance south of the border checkpoint. From there to the Kleine See where our people take us to Salzburg. In Salzburg, Lisa has a doctor ready for the operation on your face."

Borbach ran a finger over some of the scars on his face.

"I will miss these," he said. "Heinz, you have thought of everything. You have always been a fine SS officer. Perhaps you, too, can make it to South America someday."

"*Danke*, Father Franz," Holtzmann said. "We will stay in Salzburg. You will get your new *Kennkarte*, Lisa has arranged everything. Salzburg will be full with tourists at this time of the year—it will be quite safe for us to move around. From there we go to Innsbruck, to the Brenner Pass. Here we meet a new contact who will take us into Italy and to the port of Livorno. With any luck at all, you should be in South America within a month."

"You have done good work here, Heinz," Borbach said. He tried to force a smile on his face but it did not work. "You have done well. How are we situated with . . . with money?"

"We had some Ami cigarettes and Ami dollars, and they worked wonders in setting this all up," Holtzmann said.

"Good. And luck helps, too," Borbach said. "We are going to need more of that, much more. The Amis—I do not worry so much about them. They are not the most intelligent people in the world. They have passed me through several checkpoints after I told them I was working for

Daimler-Benz on a mission of finding new locations for reestablishing their business. They even wished me good luck. No, it is not the Amis—it is our fellow Germans we must watch. They are so anxious to please their new masters, the Allies, they will do anything. These days our countrymen tend to shoot first and ask questions later. It is sad, they have become real *schweine.*"

He checked his watch. He looked at me.

"How long will it take your friend to reach Bergdorf?"

"It will take him over three hours, maybe four," the Pole answered for me.

I knew Anton could get to Bergdorf much faster than that, and I was sure the Pole knew that. I saw what he was trying to do.

"Then, if he can find someone to believe his story, it will take at least another hour for the police to get up here, if they come by vehicle . . . if they come at all. We have plenty of time."

Borbach seem pleased with what he heard.

"Good . . . we shall have time for a quick lunch before we depart. Is there anything to eat in this little mountain *gasthaus*?"

"I brought up some bread along with American K rations, you know, their combat rations," the Pole said and went to a rucksack near the back wall of the bunker.

"*Ach, ya*, that is good," Borbach said. He sighed. "This is one thing the Amis have done well—they put out some decent food. Much better than that garbage the English fed me in their jail." He opened the canned meat in the ration, smelled it, then tasted it. "*Ya*—this is much better."

He ate rapidly and then lit one of the cigarettes from the small packet in the ration. He inhaled deeply.

"*Prima*," he said. "First class."

He got up and began poking around the bunker, inspecting every corner of it, as if playing war and wondering how well the fortification would stand up.

Once he looked back into the tunnel, at me, and gave me a long and hard look. I tried not to look at that face. Instead I looked at the Pole.

Back in the bunker Borbach turned to Holtzmann and Braun. The three of them spoke rapidly in German, so fast I could not understand what they were saying. But the Pole understood. He turned to me with a strange look on his face. He was pale.

I was sure he had understood their conversation.

"Can you walk . . . or run, any?" he asked me in a whisper.

I had been sweating with fear ever since we had returned to the bunker. Now, at the Pole's question, my heart began to pound so loud I was afraid they could all hear it. A heavy feeling grew in my stomach.

"A little," I answered. I knew what the Pole had planned for us. I tried hard to forget the pain in my ankle.

"We've got to get out of here," the Pole said quietly. "Borbach has made up his mind. We are a burden to him. He will kill us."

Chapter 16

Anton reached the edge of the woods, a few hundred meters short of the Alpen Rose. He was tired. He had run all the way from the bunker.

As soon as he cleared the woods he saw the man approaching from the gasthaus. The man stopped him.

"Be you coming from the bunker, lad?" he asked. He had a strange accent that Anton could not place.

Anton did not immediately answer, he was too winded.

"Ya," he said when he had caught his breath, "There is trouble up there."

He thought of the message he was supposed to give the sergeant major. He was sure this strange man with the strange accent worked for the Americans. As far as he knew he was working on the PX robbery.

"The White Gander sent me to get help. He's in trouble . . . said the Butcher was already there."

The stranger put his arm on Anton's shoulder.

"Lad, get to the colonel . . . get the sergeant major. Tell them we need the patrol immediately. Run like the devil himself is after you."

Anton nodded. He began to run again. He had to reach the Kaserne to get help for Herr Schreiber and Norman.

He looked back once. The man with the strange accent was disappearing into the woods, headed into the direction of the bunker.

• • •

The Pole motioned me to come closer.

"Go out that door," he whispered. "Go to your right, away from the bunker. Run like hell for that grove of trees—and pray. I'll be right behind you."

I eased away from the cot, jumped, and with all my strength I dashed for the door.

The blinding light of full daylight stunned me, but my fear pushed me forward to the stand of trees beyond the tunnel door. I expected to hear a shot any moment, and to feel the hot searing pain as a bullet tore into me. This was no game I was playing with some friend, this was for real, this was a run for my life. I ignored the pain in my ankle and hurtled forward in my effort to reach the safety of the woods along the trail and the gully.

The Pole, right on my heels, kept crowding me forward. He was running for his life, too.

"Faster," he yelled. "We've got to get to the gully."

I was going as fast as I could. My leg was going numb. I had a quick second thought about the wisdom of us running for safety. Maybe we should have remained in the bunker—maybe we should have sweat it out—take a chance that Borbach's gang would not shoot us?

No—the Pole had been right. Staying in the bunker meant certain death. Running was a slim chance, but it was the only chance we had. I saw what they had done to Herr Schreiber—they would do even worse to the Pole and to me. We were a burden to Borbach and we had to be eliminated.

If we could get away, we might have a chance to reach Bergdorf and there we would be safe.

I tried even harder to keep ahead of the smiling Pole, limping and jumping, trying to reach the thicker woods.

We reached the denser brush when I heard the first shot. It made a sharp cracking sound as it snapped over our heads and slammed into a tree.

Then another shot. I did not hear the snap of the bullet passing over us.

It had found a target.

Behind me, the Pole let out a yell.

"Damn it!" he gasped, "Damn it all." He had taken the bullet.

I turned to look and in that instant I crashed into a tree and stumbled to the ground.

The Pole lay on his back, clutching a leg. Above the knee, his trousers were turning red

"Keep going, Cantrell, " he urged me. "You got a chance . . . keep going."

I pulled to my feet. A short way up the hill was Holtzmann, carrying a carbine. He would reach us in moments.

I didn't know what to do. I did not want to leave the Pole. I had begun to trust him. Sepp Borbach would kill him, of that I was sure.

The Pole could have made good his escape had it not been for me. He had been slowed by me, and he had shielded me. Now he lay wounded. I could not leave him.

It was too late anyway, for Holtzmann came charging out of the bush, his carbine pointed at me.

"Sit down and stay down," he barked. He had a wild look on his face, the look of a hunter who has cornered his prey. "If you move, I will kill you right here."

He would do that. I was sure.

Braun, also armed with a carbine, ran up.

"Get the Polack on his feet," Holtzmann ordered. "I want him standing when I shoot him."

"*Nein* . . . we better take him into the bunker," Braun said. "There may be people in the woods around here . . . they may have already heard us. In the bunker, it is better." Holtzmann stared at Braun. He did not like taking orders from his companion.

"You may be right," he reluctantly acknowledged. "We'll do it in the bunker. Borbach . . . Father Franz may want to do the honors himself."

Braun pulled me to my feet and tried to get the Pole into a standing position, but he could not stand and crumpled back to the ground.

Braun prodded his carbine into the Pole's back. "You will have to crawl," he said. "And you—"

He waved his gun at me. "You get in front of him," he ordered. "If you start running, I will blow you to pieces."

I began to hobble back to the bunker. Behind me the Pole crawled, dragging his wounded leg behind him and giving a grunting moan with each move.

I was in a daze. This was all unreal. This must be the way a condemned man must feel on his way to his execution. I was sure it would all end in the bunker. Holtzmann would shoot me, along with Schreiber and the Pole, just like a hunter shooting a wounded animal.

The Pole sprawled flat on his face and lay there, motionless. I did not know if he was really that weak—or was he again stalling for time?

Braun knelt beside him.

"We stop for a quick rest," he said. He motioned to me. "And you, you *dumme Junge*, sit down."

He sounded almost friendly. At least he didn't snarl, as Holtzmann did when he spoke. Holtzmann was nowhere in sight, perhaps he was already in the bunker.

Braun was right. I had been stupid. Anton and I should have recognized the danger that was swirling all around us. And we should have run fast and far.

But we didn't. Why? Sergeant Jimmy was right—we were just too dumb.

The heaviness in my stomach forced its way out, and I threw up, there on the ground.

Braun looked at me but said nothing.

The Pole was buying extra time, I was sure of that. Maybe I could stall even more, if I could only think how . . .

I was sure Anton and help should be on the way by now— if nothing had happened to Anton. With luck—a great amount of luck—we might survive until he returned with help.

It was a very dim hope.

Chapter 17

Sergeant Major Cantrell took the call from the MP guard stationed at the front gate of the Kaserne.

"Sarge, we've got a German kid here who says he has to see the colonel or you. Says he has a message from a White Gander, whoever that is. The kid says he is Anton Brandstetter."

Sergeant Cantrell felt his heart jump. This was like the beginning of a firefight in combat, and it gave him a heavy feeling in his stomach.

"I'm on my way," he yelled into the phone, "Alert the security patrol. Full combat gear."

He made a conscious effort to remain calm as he hurried to the colonel's office.

Colonel Dearborn was out inspecting training, the secretary told him.

"Tell the old man the Butcher is already here—I'm on the way with the security patrol."

As Cantrell reached the front gate, Anton ran out and stood in his way.

"Sir—White Gander is in trouble and needs help. The Butcher came early. They are at the bunker up on Edelweiss."

"Where is Norman? I thought he was with you at the Alpen Rose."

"He is at the bunker," Anton said quickly. "His leg was sore . . . he couldn't run . . ."

He did not like the look that came over the sergeant major's face.

The security patrol leader came up for instructions.

"Get up to the bunker and surround it. I'll meet you up there," Cantrell said. "Borbach must not reach Austria. But be really careful—my son is a prisoner in that bunker."

He jumped into his Jeep and shot out of the Kaserne gate. He was well under way before he noticed that Anton was in the Jeep with him.

• • •

Holtzmann took command the moment we got back into the bunker. He immediately ordered the Pole to one of the cots.

The Pole seemed to understand—Holtzmann was itching to shoot him and me. He groaned and struggled to a cot.

Holtzmann cut a length of wire from the communication wire drum and wired the helpless Pole to the cot railing, first by his hands and then by his feet.

"Polack, we just want to keep you from wandering," Holtzmann laughed.

Then he grabbed me and pushed me to the floor beside the cot.

"You sit there . . . understand? If I see you moving around the tunnel, I will shoot you, right then and there. Got that?"

I nodded. I was too scared to speak.

Holtzmann returned to the main part of the bunker, where Sepp Borbach sat waiting.

"Father Franz, we have the birds back in the cage," he reported.

I felt I was in a frightening, dreamlike world, a horrible nightmare. Next to me was the smiling Pole, tied like a hog, ready for butchering. A few feet beyond him lay the beaten and bloody Forstmeister Schreiber. I wished for the nightmare to end, but I almost passed out as I realized that when it ended, it would be the end of me, too.

I now understood why the Pole had warned Anton and me about not climbing Edelweiss today. And I was the reason that the Pole had been recaptured. Without me, he could have escaped, I was sure. But he had protected me and that slowed him down, so that now he was here, tied up and facing death—because of me. And with me.

That Pole is one brave man, I thought, and I had put him in jeopardy.

Borbach and his two aides began talking, speaking in German, but I could hear and understand everything they said.

"This is the way I see it now," Borbach said. "We must accept that the other boy will soon reach Bergdorf. The Amis will be on their way up here shortly after that. I had hoped we would be able to speed a few hours at our little spa here, but that is now impossible. We cannot even wait for darkness. We shall have to take our chances in daylight, but the border is not far. If we stay in the woods, we can make it."

"Yes, we can do it," Holtzmann said. "Joachim and I know the way—we crossed the border without any trouble the other night. Do not worry about the border police, we know how to get around them."

Borbach's reply came loud and clear. "I do not intend to get caught in here by the Amis," he proclaimed. "If they catch me, I am a dead man. I will go down fighting if that becomes necessary, and so will you. I promise you I shall stop at nothing to get out of Germany."

It was terrifying to listen to him shout.

I heard no comment from Braun. He had been quiet since he brought us back to the bunker.

"Someone is coming!" Holtzmann suddenly yelled. He jammed a magazine of bullets into his carbine. "I hear motors down on the road."

I heard it, too. From far down the road came the growling of many motors—Jeep motors. They growled as they left the Garmisch-Partenkirchen highway and in a low gear began their climb up the slope.

"The Amis!" Borbach exploded. "We have no time left, we must move fast. The border is not that far. We go through the woods on the other side of this bunker and with a little luck, we can make it to the border."

"And our guests, what about them?" Holtzmann asked.

"*Ya.* Unfortunately, they know too much about this whole operation. We'll have to eliminate the two men. The boy goes with us, he is a kind of insurance."

"Herr *Sturmbahnfuhrer,*" Holtzmann answered, sounding very military. "The young Ami cannot walk. He has a broken or sprained ankle, he will just hold us back."

Borbach did not take long to solve this new problem.

"Eliminate him, too, *Hauptsturmfuhrer* Holtzmann, take care of it."

"Of course Herr *Sturmbahnfuhrer,*" Holtzmann snapped out. "It shall be done. *Scharfuhrer* Braun, carry out the commander's order."

It was all very military. They even began to address each other by their military titles. I guess in their twisted minds this was just another battle to be fought and won. And they would fight to the end. "Oh, Lord," the smiling Pole whispered. It sounded like a prayer. "That is the security patrol . . . let's hope they get up here and do it right."

He began struggling with the wires that bound him to the cot.

"Quick, get me loose," he ordered.

I snapped out of the paralyzing trance that had gripped me and struggled to untie him.

Chapter 18

Joachim Braun heard the motors and he knew they were Jeeps. The Amis were coming.

He also knew that Borbach and Holtzmann would never surrender without a fight. He was sure they were ready for everyone to die, if it became necessary, here in this godforsaken bunker.

Braun had long regretted that he had agreed to come out of Austria with that maniac Holtzmann. He had known him only briefly in those last days of the war when their Waffen SS division had been cut to pieces by the Americans. He and Holtzmann had escaped and gone into hiding in Austria.

"The Reich will be reborn, and they will need us again," Holtzmann had said. Braun was not so sure that the Third Reich would be reborn, nor did he want it to be. He was glad he had survived the war after being forced to join the SS just because somebody thought he looked like what an SS man should look like.

Let Holtzmann have his dream of a new Reich. Braun's dreams centered on going home to Bremerhaven and the nearby village of Bederkesa. There, on the shores of the beautiful Bederkesa See he loved so much, there his beloved Hedi and his son, Guenther, waited for him. He had not seen them for a long time.

Braun had sometimes thought of turning himself over to the Americans and getting his discharge from the German military. He did not think he would have any trouble in that. He had not committed the crimes that Borbach and Holtzmann had committed.

He was still upset that Holtzmann had ordered him to go along to the highway to meet Borbach. Someone should have remained behind to guard the bunker, to scare away these boys if they returned.

Today, encountering the young Ami boy on the slope, a strong yearning grabbed him. The young Ami reminded him so much of his own Guenther. Braun wanted to go home.

• • •

Everything was swirling about me. I knew what lay ahead. My little game of look-for-the-bunker-and-find-the-cigarettes was coming to an end. The security patrol would never reach us in time.

Thoughts of Herr Schreiber and the smiling Pole shot into my mind. They would die along with me.

A thought of Father flashed into my mind, and I let out a sob. In that moment I loved my father more than I ever had. I had never appreciated that he loved me, that he needed me as much as I needed him.

"*Na, Junge*, it is time."

It was Joachim Braun. He came from the bunker, holding a carbine pointed straight at me. In the half darkness, the muzzle looked huge.

I became numb. I just stared at the carbine.

"How old are you, *Junge*?" Braun asked.

"Thirteen," I squeaked out. I could not think, my answer came out automatically.

"*Na*—the same age as my Guenther."

His voice had softened, and he shook his head.

"This is such nonsense," he said softly.

He looked at his carbine and I saw his finger tighten on the trigger. I thought he raised the carbine higher, but I was not sure because the weapon barked and flame shot out of the muzzle. I heard a sharp crack and smelled gunpowder.

I crumpled and fell to the floor. A dark haze began to cover me and I wondered when the pain of the bullet would come.

But there was no pain, no final darkness, only the dizziness that came with my fear.

"You have been executed," Braun said. He said it in a low and gentle voice, almost like that of a father speaking to a son who had been bad.

He fired two more rapid shots into the ceiling.

"You have all been shot," he said, smiling at the Pole. He put down the carbine and jumped for the rear door. At the door he turned and gave me a smile. It was a friendly smile, almost as if he was asking for forgiveness. Then he was gone.

The carbine lay on the floor in front of me. Slowly, life returned to my mind. I felt no pain, I saw no blood. No bullet had touched me. Braun had spared me. He had spared all of us. His shots had all plowed into the roof of the tunnel, over our heads.

Cold sweat soaked me. But I began breathing again.

"Quick, get the carbine," the Pole said. "If the others come back here, you shoot. Don't look to me for advice, just shoot to kill . . . and try to untie me."

He struggled to free himself.

A glimmer of hope surged through me. If I got the carbine, and if the Pole got loose, he could shoot the two remaining members of the Borbach gang.

I picked the weapon up. I fought back a temptation to run for the door. But I didn't run. I saw the look of fear on the Pole's face and I heard, behind me, the voice of Holtzmann.

"That *Schwein* Braun. He's betrayed us. He's going over to the Amis," he yelled angrily, loud enough so that Borbach in the front of the bunker could hear. "That traitor. Now I will have to finish the job myself."

Chapter 19

Chris Stuart heard two shots coming from the woods ahead of him. They came from the direction of the bunker.

He stopped. He had been running ever since he got the message from Anton.

There were no more shots. He patted the revolver in the holster and began running again.

His friend, the American agent, was in trouble up there and he had to get to him before Borbach discovered who he was.

Cantrell, that American boy, was also up there. He did not want to think of what those two shots might mean.

He kept running and then, at last, he found himself close enough to see the bunker. He drew his revolver.

In the same moment he heard three more shots coming from inside the bunker.

• • •

Holtzmann looked at me with that sneer on his face. He laughed, an ugly barking laugh.

Suddenly the memory of that pheasant hunter in Iowa shot into my mind—the same sneer, the same look of a man who enjoys killing for the sake of killing.

Now I was the bird who was going to be killed.

The pheasant in Iowa had been wounded and he had died. Now I was the pheasant who was going to be shot, and I would die.

A strong anger fought my fear for control of my mind. I had no conscious thought of what I was doing. The carbine was in my hands, and my finger began hugging the trigger. It was all instinct. I began pulling the trigger, and I could not stop. Again and again I pulled the trigger and each time the semiautomatic gun answered my command. I squeezed off shot after shot in a haze of wild anger.

A look of surprise came to Holtzmann's face and froze there. His eyes opened wide. He tried to point his weapon at me, but it dropped from his hands, as if he no longer had the strength to hold it. The recoil of my gun jerked me out of my hypnotic state, but I fired again and again. I could not stop. It was as if some other person was inside of me, pulling the trigger, controlling the action.

At last I stopped firing.

Holtzmann was still on his feet, that look of frightened surprise frozen on his face. His eyes, still wide open, stared as if he could not believe what had happened. Slowly, he began to topple. His legs crumpled under him and he slid to the floor and lay still.

I stood over him, ready to fire again, if he as much as quivered. A surge of exhilaration swept over me. It was like hitting a winning home run with the score tied in the last inning of a game of baseball. I wanted to yell and dance.

A sudden shout from the Pole brought me back to face the real world that still existed around me.

"Great, Norman," he yelled. "Now get Borbach before . . ."

I had forgotten about Sepp Borbach. I didn't even know how many rounds, if any, were left in my carbine magazine.

I whirled, ready to fire again. I found myself staring into the bore of a pistol held in the huge hand of Sepp Borbach.

The Pole had freed himself, and he reached out and kicked my feet from under me. I fell flat on the ground. In the same instant I fired another round.

I saw one of Borbach's legs slowly turning red. He lowered his pistol and pointed it at me. At that moment I heard the slow but steady chug-chug of a gun firing over my head.

"Stay down, Norman," the Pole yelled.

"*Yetzt ist schluss*, Herr Borbach," someone with a heavy accent said. "It is the end of the road."

Stepping over me was the stocky figure of Christopher Stuart, the special investigator of the PX robbery. He held a revolver and fired shot after shot into Borbach.

Borbach hit the floor like a toppled tree and lay still. He still held his pistol in his hand, but Stuart kicked it out of his hand.

"It is over," Stuart said quietly. It sounded almost like a prayer of thanks. "It is over."

A couple of GIs, armed with submachine guns, burst through the door.

"Take him," a familiar voice ordered. "Search him—his boots, his jacket, everything. Don't ever take your eyes off him, he is still very dangerous."

It was Father.

He dropped to his knees beside me on the floor.

"You okay, Normie?" he asked several times. "Are you okay?" He put an arm around me and held me tightly.

I could not speak, so I nodded. I reached out to him and held on to him. The fear drained out of me, and I began to sob. Slowly at first, then fast, hard sobs shook me. I didn't care who saw or heard me. It was all over. I was with Father. I was safe. The nightmare was over.

"You did great, Normie, I couldn't have done better. You did great," Father said.

Anton came from somewhere and rushed to my side.

"You okay?" he asked as he grabbed my hand. He looked as if he felt bad about something. I didn't know if it was because he had to leave me behind—or was it because he had missed out on all the big action in the bunker?

"I'm fine, I'm fine," I told him. I took his hand. "Thank you for getting here so fast."

Stuart stood over the cot where the Pole sat.

"I thought you Limey would never get here," the Pole said with a grin on his face. He had to struggle, but it was a real grin. "I almost didn't make it, you know."

"Yes, that I can see," Stuart said. "I should never have left you alone to handle a big show like this. It takes someone with a real knack for this kind of work."

Stuart, too, was grinning. I wondered—they had both come so close to death, but they could still laugh about it— brave men.

"We can thank young Cantrell, here," the Pole said. "Without him you'd have found some bodies in here."

Anton uncovered Herr Schreiber. The Forstmeister was conscious. Tears rolled down his cheeks as he saw that help was here at last.

"*Danke*, Anton, you and Norman, *danke*," he said in a very tired voice.

By this time a couple of army medics had come into the bunker and, after taking a quick look at me, immediately went to work on Herr Schreiber. They placed him on a stretcher and carried him down to a waiting ambulance that had followed the security patrol.

The medics checked out the Pole, who, except for the wound in his leg, seemed ready to get going again on some new adventure.

Me, I was ready to go, too—home to Bergdorf.

Chapter 20

Father Otto leaned over the edge of the Goose Pond and watched his white feathered friends chase the bits of bread he tossed them.

Sometimes he wondered about all the bread people were giving the geese when sometimes there was not that much bread to spare. But these feathered friends were as much a part of his church as his regular parishioners and they deserved the food they got.

"They are always hungry, Padre."

It was Colonel Dearborn, who had taken a seat on one of the benches.

"Ya, that is but true, Colonel, but then—hunger is quite common in the world today."

"True. But I have come to see you, Padre, about a hunger of a different kind. One of my young troopers, Norman Cantrell, is having a problem. That happening in the Edelweiss bunker was tough enough, but now he has a guilty feeling for killing a man."

"I have heard that," Father Otto said. Frau Weidl had spoken to him about her concern for the young American. "That is a heavy load, especially for someone like Norman."

"I could ask my own chaplain to look into this, but he is new over here, and Padre, from what I hear, Norman has a lot of confidence in you."

Father Otto was pleased. It was good to know that he had reached Norman. The young American was a fine boy who had

done much to help bridge the gap between Germans and
Americans in postwar Bergdorf.

"I shall do what I can, Colonel," he promised. "I shall see him
this evening."

The colonel stood up. He extended his hand.

"Thank you, Padre. We must find a way to help him handle
his load. Anything you can do, I shall consider as a personal
favor."

"I shall do my best," Father Otto promised.

He knew it was going to be difficult.

● ● ●

It was over. The manmade storm that had slammed
into our little community was gone, but it left behind people who had been hurt.

I was one of them. At first I had only the countless
questions as I tried to fit all the pieces of the Borbach puzzle together. Father helped me with that.

I had already figured out that the smiling Pole was not
a big-time black market dealer from the DP camp. Father
said he was a Lieutenant Jan Gudowski, a U.S. Army intel-
ligence agent who had teamed with Christopher Stuart,
former British commando, to recapture Sepp Borbach.

"There never was a PX robbery for Chris Stuart to
investigate. We gave Lieutenant Gudowski some cigarettes
and a lot of money, and we raised a lot of hell to set him up
as a big-time operator who could help Borbach make his
escape into Austria."

Now I understood why Lieutenant Gudowski had tried
so hard to keep Anton and me away from the bunker. We
were in the way, we could mess up the whole operation, we
could get hurt or killed. He wanted to keep us safely at
home, out of the way of the storm that Borbach would
bring.

But we ignored his warnings. Why? Why did we insist
on finding that bunker on Edelweiss Mountain?

That was easy to answer. Anton was fed up with the constant harassment by the police. He was intent on proving his family had no part in the PX robbery. And I did not like what they did to Anton and his family, I wanted to show him that I, his American friend, was standing with him, even if my own army was against him. But that was not the only reason. Anton and I were excited by the lure of adventure and we let ourselves get sucked up in a storm, a storm we both were too naive and ignorant to see the dangers it was bringing.

But the Pole, knowing what the storm could bring, risked his life for us. Especially for me. I was glad that, in those final moments in the bunker, I had been able to repay the debt I owed him.

"How did Gudowski and Stuart know so much about Borbach and his plans for crossing into Austria?" I asked Father.

He did not immediately answer. When he did, he sounded hesitant.

"I am going to tell you something, Norman, that you must not ever tell anyone—not even Anton. You must promise that."

I agreed to keep my mouth shut.

"Let's just say we have a contact who was once one of Borbach's men. Now he works for us. Keep that quiet or I'm in big trouble."

That was all he ever said about a contact and I never asked for more information, nor did I ever talk about it, not even to Anton.

Father, though, had more to say about the Borbach case.

"As for you, Norman, never, never in my wildest thoughts and fears did I ever think you would get caught up in that thing," he said. He shook his head. "But I have to admit, you did a great job up there in the that bunker and . . . I am proud of you, Norman. Damn proud. And so is the colonel."

I felt great to hear that. I was grateful that Father did not give me one of his ever-ready sermons about my responsibilities as a U.S. Army dependent stationed in occupied Germany. By now I knew most of those sermons by heart.

So the pieces all slid into place, the puzzle was complete, and I had a picture of what had happened.

But for me, there were still problems connected with that nightmare in the bunker.

First, it was the dream. It was there from the start and it began to get to me. It was always the same. I was in the bunker, and someone was coming to shoot me. But it was not Braun coming to shoot me that haunted me, it was the man with the cold eyes and the frightening sneer on his face. It was Holtzmann.

In the dream, I began shooting, but my carbine did not fire. I desperately squeezed the trigger, over and over again. Nothing happened. I knew that my death was only seconds away.

Some nights the dream was a little different. I again started to shoot the moment Holtzmann aimed his weapon at me. I hugged the carbine and shot bullet after bullet into my enemy. His face turned white and he became a terrifying wide-eyed monster that refused to fall. I fired until my gun was empty, but Holtzmann still refused to fall. He should be dead, but he just stood there and looked at me with accusing eyes.

When I woke, my heart pounded like crazy and I was wet with sweat.

Frau Weidl noticed something was bothering me.

"Normie, what is it? I know something is keeping you awake."

"No no," I said quickly. I did not want to get her to worrying about me. But she had been like a mother to me and she had helped me before, maybe now she could help me again.

"Yes, Frau Weidl, I do have something bothering me," I admitted.

She sat down beside me and I told her, everything.

"And now, I feel awful. I feel guilty about killing that man," I confessed to her. The confession did little to relieve my feeling of guilt.

She hugged me and wiped tears from her eyes. She always got emotional over things, just like my mother always had before she died.

"It will go away, Normie, give it time. It will go away," she said. I wanted to believe her, but I didn't really think that would happen—it was my punishment for what I had done, for killing a man.

Frau Weidl, of course, told Father, and the next day he questioned me.

"Yes, I do have bad nightmares," I told him. "And now, on top of everything, I feel guilty about killing Holtzmann."

I felt comfortable telling my father this. There had been a time when I probably would have kept it to myself. But Father had changed and so had I. Now I felt I could talk to him and he would understand.

"Want to go to the hospital in Munich?" he asked, "They've got some doctors there that you can talk to."

"No, not that," I said. "They'll just ask me a lot of silly questions. No, let me work it out. I'll be okay."

I tried to sound confident, but how would I work things out? I didn't have the slightest idea.

A couple of days later I got more advice. I was at the Goose Pond when Colonel Dearborn's Jeep rolled up and the colonel joined me on the bench.

"Your father tells me you are having bad nights," he said. He came straight to the point. He always did that, he never sparred around, just got to the subject he wanted to discuss and that was it. He sounded very friendly, very human, not like the tough old combat-experienced commander he really was. I guess he really missed his son, who was in the States.

"Yes, sir," I said.

"Norman, those things happen all the time, especially in the military," he said and placed a hand on my shoulder.

"They will go away, believe me, they will go away. You did a brave thing up there in that bunker and I am proud of you. I am glad you are one of my troopers. You just have to hang in there. Shooting Holtzmann was something that, well, it was something which had to be done. You saved the lives of two other men, and you saved your own life. Just remember, son—you saved lives. That is a good you can take from this experience."

I had already run that around in my head a hundred times. I believed with all my heart that I had to shoot Holtzmann to save my own life and that of the smiling Pole and Herr Schreiber. The nightmares were becoming less frequent, but I could not shake that heavy feeling of guilt. I had killed a man, I, who not so long ago had sworn I would never kill any living thing. I had violated something that I so strongly believed.

And the next evening, when Father Otto came to the house, he did his best, just like the others, to help me understand things about life.

"I have seen a lot of guilt in my lifetime. So much of it is unnecessary," he told me. He had much of the same outlook as the colonel, and my father.

He was concerned and he tried hard, but in the end I still had no real answer to my problem.

And there was Anton.

"You did a real brave thing," he told me one day. That's all he ever said—he didn't offer any advice and for that I was thankful. I knew that he was concerned and that was enough for me.

And then, one day, it all came to me and I saw why I had been so willing to kill. It came to me at the Goose Pond, where I was sharing a bench with Dorothy De Jong.

Herr Schreiber sat on an adjacent bench, talking to himself. He had been coming to the Goose Pond a lot since his release from the hospital. Here he would sit for hours and talk to himself and to the geese. It got so bad, his friends called his oldest daughter, Ursula, and she came from Stuttgart to take care of him. She went with him wherever he went. It was just too dangerous to let him go out alone. The old man had a habit of just wandering away. Some said he probably thought he was still the Bergdorf Forstmeister.

That day, at the pond, Dorothy and I had been talking about Iowa and about the coming school year when we would begin high school.

Suddenly a loud cry shook us.

"*Vatti—nein! Komm heraus.*"

It was Ursula. She came out of the bakery with a bag full of bread.

"*Vatti, bitte, komm hier,*" she pleaded. "Come out of the water."

Her father was in the middle of the Goose Pond, in water up to his chest. In his hand he held bits of bread that he dished out to the smaller geese.

"My little friends, you must not let bigger ones push you away from the food," he said softy. "It is yours as much as it is theirs. Come here, I will take care of you. You are my friends, you are my little people."

Ursula looked at me, pleading for help.

I jumped up and waded into the pond until I reached the old Forstmeister. I grabbed him by an arm and said, "Come, Herr Schreiber, come with me. Your little friends have plenty to eat."

He came meekly, like a child, as I led him back to the bench. Dorothy brought some towels from the bakery, and she and Ursula and I helped the old man dry himself as best as we could.

Herr Schreiber sat huddled on the bench. He looked confused and lost. He suddenly hid his face in a towel and began to cry loud, hurting sobs that got to me. I put my arm around him and choked back my own feelings.

An insane anger gripped me. Here was Herr Schreiber crying with heartbreaking sobs, helpless as a young child. He was a very decent person, a good man who had loved the trees and birds and the animals on his beloved Edelweiss Mountain.

But now he was a crippled old man, retired from the mountain and the forest he loved, needing the help of others to see him through life. It was painful to see him cry. I saw a wrecked man who would never be able to move in the world he had known. Things would not get better for him.

My anger grew as I held tight to him. Holtzmann had done this to him. Holtzmann had beaten Herr Schreiber and left wounds that would haunt the Forstmeister the rest of his days. Holtzmann had tried to kill him. And me. And the Pole.

It was like we were a bunch of birds and Holtzmann was the hunter trying to shoot us.

Dorothy saw my anger. She knew the pain I was feeling. "You have every right to be angry. I am angry, too, at what has happened to this good man," she said. She had tears in her eyes. "You once told me a story of a hunter in Iowa who had shot a pheasant and that you were not able to save that bird's life. Well, up there in that bunker, Herr Schreiber was a wounded pheasant. The smiling Pole was a wounded pheasant, and you were a pheasant, about to be killed. That hunter tried to kill all of you. But this time the pheasant shot the hunter. Norman, it's all as simple as that. It's a sort of natural justice."

I thought of that the rest of the day and that night as I struggled with my anger, I thought of the twilight world of Herr Schreiber. I thought of the final darkness that would have fallen over him, the Pole, and me if I had not fought back.

I had fought back because I wanted to live, just as that pheasant in Iowa had wanted to live. I did this without thinking, instinctively. It was a natural law of life.

Yes, Dorothy was right—I had been the hunted pheasant and I had killed the sneering hunter. It was that simple. And as I thought of the wounded Forstmeister, I was glad I had done what I did.

The next morning, when I woke, it was like after a dark storm ends—suddenly the clouds race away and the sun shines once again. The weight of the guilt I had been carrying around inside of me begin to dissolve like snow in a warm sun.

The darkness left me and I walked in sunshine once more. I grew up that day and I saw that life is not always black and white. I had always thought that was the way it was, most of the time it really had many shades of gray. And that day I saw what true and simple and clear answer Dorothy had given me.

That day, on a bench near the Goose Pond in Bergdorf, Germany, I discovered I was in love with that girl from Iowa.

Epilogue

The bunker died in a powerful blast of fire and smoke.

First, before the explosion, German workers removed the few things of value in the bunker, mainly the cots, the drums of communication wire, and the wooden ammo boxes.

A group of U.S. Army engineers began placing explosives at key places in the bunker and in the tunnel.

At last it was time for the final act.

I was there that day, and so was Anton. Anton's father, who was the new Forstmeister for the Edelweiss Mountain woods, was there. He rode up with Colonel Dearborn.

Karl Schrieber was not there. He had turned down Colonel Dearborn's offer of a ride. Perhaps his damaged mind no longer wanted to see the bunker, or, perhaps, it no longer remembered it. Anton and I rode with Father in his Jeep. A GI engineer stopped us at a bend in the road that branched off from the Garmisch-Partenkirchen highway.

"Better hold it here," he warned. "Sometimes all kinds of rock and trees and things come down the mountain after we set off a blast. You should be okay here."

A sergeant brought wires down from the bunker, down to a safe distance from the explosion that would rip the bunker apart.

"She's about ready to go, sir," the lieutenant in charge of the crew told Colonel Dearborn. "All we've got to do is hook it up."

Anton and I got out of the Jeep and ran up to the engineer officer.

"We just want to take a last look at the bunker," I told him. "We're not going up there. We want to take a last look at it, from here, sir."

The officer nodded. He knew what had happened up there.

I looked up at the bunker. Now, more than ever, it looked like a evil-looking mushroom. But I still felt a little sad that it had to go. It was not the bunker that had caused so much trouble, it was the men who had used it.

"I am glad it will soon be kaputt," Anton said. He had his own reason for wanting that.

We looked for a few minutes, then returned to the Jeep.

"All clear," the sergeant yelled. He looked around, then yelled again: "Fire in the hole."

He rammed down the plunger. An electric charge shot through the wires to set off the explosives in the bunker.

There was a second of dead silence. Then a great burst of fire and smoke erupted on the side of the mountain. The bunker rose and seemed to hang in the air. With a deafening sound, the explosives ripped the mass of concrete and steel apart. Huge chunks of concrete and rocks settled to the ground. Some began rolling down the slope.

The ground around us shook, even as far down the road as we were. The ground trembled as rocks crashed into the woods below the bunker. They smashed into trees, and most stopped rolling. A few continued the journey all the way to the road.

The smoke began to clear, and I saw the remains of the bunker, now just large chunks of reinforced concrete scattered on the hillside. The tunnel had caved in.

But the destruction was not yet complete.

High up, in the rock field above the bunker, the ground began to move. It seemed as if the mountain was shaking itself, and with that, more waves of rock began rolling downhill. It looked as if Edelweiss Mountain wanted to help the engineers erase all signs of the big sore in its side.

The rockslide stopped. I looked up the slope. Rocks covered the remains of the bunker. A wind blew the smoke and dust away from where the bunker had been.

There was no sign that anything manmade had ever existed up there. Once more, a quiet peace settle over Edelweiss Mountain.

And the peace reached all the way down to where Anton and I stood, each lost in our own thoughts.

• • •

I go to the Goose Pond almost every day now. I sit on the bench at the edge of the pond and wait for Gabby, the senior gander of that gang of white feathered bandits, to join me.

As soon as he sees me, Gabby rushes up and waits for me to lift him onto the bench. When he has parked himself beside me, I feed him a piece of the sweet roll I bought in the bakery. He gulps it down.

Dorothy often joins us on the bench. She sometimes brings grapes for Gabby and his gang, and she is greeted with loud cries of welcome. They know she is bringing them something extra good.

Dorothy and I sit and talk about a lot of things. We talk of Iowa, and we talk of life as army dependents in Bergdorf.

After a while, when the food is all gone, Gabby gets bored with us. He is not interested in our talk. He nips me on my arm, and I help him down from the bench. He returns to the pond where he barks out orders to his gang. I wish I could understand what he is saying.

I don't mind him leaving me and Dorothy alone. I know he will be back as soon as he gets hungry again.

In the meantime, I have more time to be with the girl from Iowa.

The End